The Fourth Suit

The MAGIC MISFITS

The Fourth Suit

By Neil Patrick Harris
& Alec Azam

STORY ARTISTRY BY LISSY MARLIN

HOW-TO MAGIC ART BY KYLE HILTON

Little, Brown and Company

New York Boston

Text and illustrations copyright © 2020 by Neil Patrick Harris

Story illustrations by Lissy Marlin. How-To illustrations by Kyle Hilton.

Cover art by Lissy Marlin. Cover design by Karina Granda. Cover art copyright © 2020 by Neil Patrick Harris. Cover copyright © 2020 by Hachette Book Group, Inc.

Little, Brown and Company
Hachette Book Group
1290 Avenue of the Americas, New York, NY 10104
Visit us at LBYR.com

First Edition: September 2020

Little, Brown and Company is a division of Hachette Book Group, Inc.
The Little, Brown name and logo are trademarks of Hachette Book Group, Inc.

The publisher is not responsible for websites (or their content) that are not owned by the publisher.

Library of Congress Cataloging-in-Publication Data
Names: Harris, Neil Patrick, 1973– author. | Azam, Alec, author. | Marlin, Lissy, illustrator. | Hilton, Kyle, illustrator.
Title: The fourth suit / by Neil Patrick Harris & Alec Azam ; story artistry by Lissy Marlin ; how-to magic art by Kyle Hilton.
Description: First edition. | New York : Little, Brown and Company, 2020. | Series: The Magic Misfits ; 4 | Audience: Ages 8–12. | Summary: "The Magic Misfits confront their greatest enemy in this final story told from Ridley's point of view"— Provided by publisher.
Identifiers: LCCN 2020030157 | ISBN 9780316391955 (hardcover) | ISBN 9780316391948 (ebook) | ISBN 9780316391931 (ebook other)
Subjects: CYAC: Magic tricks—Fiction. | Hypnotism—Fiction. | Friendship—Fiction. | Mothers and daughters—Fiction. | Humorous stories.
Classification: LCC PZ7.1.H3747 Fou 2020 | DDC [Fic] —dc23
LC record available at https://lccn.loc.gov/2020030157

ISBNs: 978-0-316-39195-5 (hardcover), 978-0-316-39194-8 (ebook), 978-0-316-70334-5 (int'l)

Printed in the United States of America

LSC-C

10 9 8 7 6 5 4 3 2

To David:
the Other Mr. Harris,
and the center ring of our family circus

TABLE OF CONTENTS

STOP! HALT! WHO GOES THERE?

Oh, it's *you* again!

Thank goodness.

I was here in the dark, when I felt a presence and was worried that someone was reading this who shouldn't be. That's not to say *you* shouldn't be reading this. You should most definitely be reading this.

You don't mind waiting a moment while I turn on a light, do you?

There we are. Much better.

I apologize for my jumpiness. Thinking about everything that is forthcoming has made me slightly anxious. But being here with you, of all people…well, I'm quite happy you're here to keep me company as we begin the fourth—and final—tale of our adventurous Magic Misfits.

As I'm sure you're aware, the conclusion to an epic chronicle can be nerve-racking. And after learning all you have about Carter, Leila, Theo, Ridley, Olly, Illy, Ozzy, Izzy, Dante, the Other Mister Vernon, Presto, Change-O, Top Hat, and Theo's doves, I'm sure you're as worried about them as I've been. (Presto, Change-O, Top Hat, and the Doves sounds like a stupendous name for a band. Just sayin'.) You must be itching to find out how things have progressed for each of them since the disastrous end to our previous tale.

I'll admit, I've shed a tear or two myself at the thought of Vernon's Magic Shop lying in ruins. All those tricks, all that joy, all that sparkle burned to a crisp thanks to the villain Kalagan, who still lurks about the streets of Mineral Wells, watching from the shadows as our Misfits begin another year of school. I'm sure he's only biding his time until he's ready to strike again….

Eep!

My apologies. I thought I heard a noise. Perhaps I shall turn on another light.

Now, allow me to catch you up on everything you need to know going into the coming adventure. The Magic Misfits are comprised of Carter Locke, who makes things vanish; Leila Vernon, who escapes from tight spots; Theo Stein-Meyer, an aficionado of levitation; Ridley Larsen, a tinkerer proficient in the magical art of transformation; and Olly and Izzy Golden, gymnastic, musical comedians who keep their friends laughing no matter the circumstances.

Of course, who could laugh when a showdown with a powerful magician bent on revenge is imminent? I'm not sure I could. Nevertheless, you *must* read on. The only thing left for me to share with you now is...

HOW TO
Read This Book!

I know, I know. At this point in the game, this little section seems redundant. Yes?

You already know how to read this book!

So allow me to refresh: There are parts of this book that tell a story. And in between those story sections, I will share with you a few magic tricks. If you've been with us since the beginning, and if you've been paying attention and practicing all that I've taught you so far, you *may* have realized that these tricks are leading up to something *big*. A grand finale, if you will!

So, for the first time, I shall ask that you *not* skip our magic lessons as you read Ridley's story. You've already learned and practiced so many magical tricks that you mustn't give up now (though my guess is that you're no quitter and that you'll want to study them and practice, practice, practice until you're quite perfect)!

Are you ready?

Then please do turn the page!

ONE

Ridley Larsen's life was a locomotive barreling toward an unknown destination. The events of the past summer made her feel like she was moving through a dark tunnel, one filled with smoke and the occasional screaming whistle, and if she came upon a sharp curve, she feared she might come completely off the tracks.

On this particular morning in early October, Ridley was traveling with a woman her mother had hired to take over Ridley's homeschooling, Ms. Parkly, and the reason she was thinking about her life as a locomotive was because she and Ms. Parkly were literally riding in a train. The wheels of Ridley's chair were strapped to a spot beside one of the windows, and the outside world whizzed by, the foliage of early autumn blurring with the crisp and slanted morning light.

Her teacher sat in the row in front of her. Facing backward, the woman was focused on Ridley's splayed hands. "Do it again! Again!" Ms. Parkly squeaked with excitement.

Ridley was performing a magic trick for her teacher. "Watch closely now," she said, amused that Ms. Parkly sounded like an amazed little kid visiting Mr. Vernon's old magic shop. Ridley held out her hands, empty palms facing upward. She curled her fingers into fists. "Pick a hand."

Ms. Parkly pointed to Ridley's left.

Ridley covered her left fist with her right hand and then gave them both a rough shake. When she opened her left hand again, a small illustration of the word *nope* had appeared, printed onto her palm. Ms. Parkly laughed.

"Wrong choice," said Ridley, now opening her right hand to reveal a small silver screw in her palm. Ms. Parkly offered quiet, excited applause.

Ridley smiled, an odd sensation given the way she'd

felt the past several months. After the disaster at the Mineral Wells Talent Show, and the destruction of Vernon's Magic Shop, pieces of Ridley's life felt like they'd been transformed as well: her town, of course; her relationships with her closest friends; her beliefs about how life should be. About how *she* should be. Calm? Tough? More trusting? Or someone who always trusts her gut?

Ridley wondered what her friends would prefer, especially after the way she'd treated them lately— insisting on her own way, barreling forward without a thought for everyone's safety. Still, she'd had the best of intentions. Didn't her friends know that?

(Ah, a good question. Have you ever felt uncertain about who you are? About the *real* you? I know I have. Come to think of it, I've never revealed who *I* am…so perhaps I should stop asking questions!)

"I don't know how you do it, Ridley," Ms. Parkly said. "You impress me."

Ridley shrugged. "If I had a nickel for every time someone said that, I'd be rich." Then she chuckled. "But probably cranky from all the bags of loose change lying around."

Ridley's mother had hired Helena Parkly to be

Ridley's homeschool teacher at the
beginning of September, just
before Ridley's father had left
on one of his long sales trips.
The teacher was a thin woman,
slightly taller than Mrs. Larsen.
Other than her strawberry-
blond bob, Ms. Parkly dressed
like someone twenty years
older than she actually was—
often in a buttoned-up blouse
and a scratchy wool jacket and skirt
that draped just past her knees.
When Ridley had first met her
teacher, she'd thought the woman

looked professional and intelligent. But she also knew
that looks could be deceiving. For one thing, the
woman was extremely clumsy, constantly knocking
things over or tripping. And very easily distracted by
Ridley's simplest magic tricks.

One of the first things that Ms. Parkly had done
after learning about Ridley's knack for invention was
to sign her up for a regional young inventors' fair in
nearby Bell's Landing, where the two were traveling

now. If it had been a ploy to win Ridley's favor, it had worked. After years of tinkering and imagining impressive machines with little to show for it, Ridley was finally going to prove to herself that her hobby was worthwhile. Useful.

Her project was about transforming shared spaces so that anyone could navigate them with ease. After brainstorming for many hours with her father before he'd left on his latest trip, Ridley had developed a manual crank system that would allow her to move up and down the stairs in their house without having to leave her chair. Ropes, pulleys, wheels, and cogs would temporarily tilt the steps into a ramp formation. Along with a display board that described the mechanics of the device, Ridley had brought along a miniature proof-of-concept model, both of which were packed into the bag lying on the floor beside Ridley's chair.

"Will you teach me that trick?" Ms. Parkly asked hopefully. "How'd you do it?"

"I should *probably* start thinking about my invention presentation," Ridley answered pointedly. She was most definitely not going to reveal the mechanics of her trick to someone she'd only known a month, no matter what the teacher had done for her.

Ms. Parkly smiled. "Ah, you're right. I'm distracting you."

"It's fine. I just need to get back to work." Ridley pulled her notebook from the compartment in the armrest of her chair and flipped it open. She focused on the pages until she saw Ms. Parkly turn to sit back down, though the teacher first had to disentangle the cuff of her blouse from a loose screw sticking out of her seat.

"Oof!" Ms. Parkly said as her sleeve came loose and she landed with a *whump!* She let out a strange little giggle, and for the second time that morning, Ridley found herself unexpectedly smiling.

✦ ✦ ✦

With its cobblestone streets and century-old architecture, Bell's Landing had a similar charm to Ridley's hometown, though it was much larger. The buildings were taller, the parks wider. The theaters seated more people. The smokestacks and engines of multiple factories produced products even faster. The stores had more departments and sold a wider variety of goods.

Instead of a resort on a nearby rise, like the Grand

Oak back home, Bell's Landing had Bell College, which was located in the flatlands beside the winding river that connected this city to Mineral Wells. The structures that formed Bell College were built of granite and marble and, in a most impressive illusion, the buildings appeared to be held up by vines of ivy that were just starting to turn a reddish hue in the early October shift of sunlight.

After they'd stopped for lunch, Ridley and Ms. Parkly made their way to the college's front gate—a black wrought-iron monstrosity decorated with blackbirds, which gave off an aura more of intimidation than of education. It took a lot to intimidate Ridley, though, so she wheeled quickly through the college's entrance, her bag in her lap. One would never have guessed that her heart was a steam engine pounding in her chest. Ms. Parkly followed rather wide-eyed behind her.

Across the quad, Hampshire Hall was a great gray structure, with tall windows, a red-slate roof, and an impossibly large staircase leading up to a front door.

"Follow me," Ridley said. "And watch out for that." She pointed at a potted plant someone had knocked onto the bluestone path. Ms. Parkly nodded her thanks, though Ridley still heard a quiet "Ouch!" and the tinkle of broken pottery as she sped to the side of the hall. There she found a door that was level with the lawn. She released a clasp on the underside of her chair's armrest and grabbed the hook apparatus that she'd attached for moments like this. Pulling on one end of it, Ridley felt the hook arm extend and click into place. She swung it toward the door and seized the handle. Moving her thumb along the switch at the arm's base, she tightened the hook, twisted her wrist, and pulled.

The door swung outward. Ridley inched her chair forward and caught the door with her footrest, propping it open. She then released the hook device, reattached it to the underside of the chair's arm, and turned to Ms. Parkly. "In we go," she said.

"Why, thank you," her teacher replied, giving that strange little giggle again and stumbling slightly as she moved past Ridley.

After blindly navigating the snaking halls inside Hampshire Hall for several minutes, Ridley encountered some kids who were carrying strange-looking gadgets. "This way," she told her teacher. Ridley followed the kids to a giant classroom, inside of which many tables were arranged in rows. A line had formed at a desk just inside the door, and three adults in stiff tweed suits sat behind it, waving participants forward.

Ms. Parkly started to say, "I'll just check us i—" But Ridley shook her head sharply, hurrying forward.

"Ridley Larsen, here for the inventors' fair." She tried to sound cool and collected, though her nerves were buzzing.

One of the tweed-suited adults handed her a slip of paper with a number on it. "Welcome. Your spot is in the row closest to the windows. Can't miss it."

"*Thank yooo-oou,*" Ms. Parkly said in an odd sing-song voice, bumping into the registration table as she passed, causing a loud screech as its legs scraped the marble floor. The tweed-suited people grimaced.

"*Soooor-ry!*" she said again, smoothing her skirt and hurrying after Ridley, who was already well ahead.

They passed by other participants. Glancing at their poster boards, Ridley noticed a variety of project titles: THE AUTOMATIC PAGE TURNER, THE EASY RAKE WITH ATTACHED LEAF-COLLECTION BAG, THE REMOTE-CONTROL LIGHT SWITCH, THE LOST MARBLE LOCATOR. She wasn't sure what some of them were, but it was possible one of them would blow her invention right out of the water.

"Are you as nervous as I am?" Ms. Parkly asked. The little laugh again.

"I'm fine!" Ridley answered, much louder than she'd meant to. Her teacher's odd mannerisms were getting to her. She tried to fix it with a wide grin, but then worried that might make it worse, so she made her face go blank, which she was sure only made her look like a creep.

"Good!" Ms. Parkly replied, pink faced. "Me too! I'm actually not nervous at all. I don't even know why I said that."

"It's all right," Ridley said quietly. The steam engine in her chest went ka-*chunk*-ka-*chunk*-ka-*chunk*. Maybe it would help to just admit it. "I actually *am* a tiny bit anxious."

She plopped the large bag atop the table and zipped it open. Within seconds, she'd removed her poster board and propped it up for all to see. The red title at the top stood out: THE TRANSFORMING STAIRCASE. Below were the various blueprints and diagrams that Ridley had put together, as well as drawings of the finished product and a detailed description. Ridley then laid out the pieces of her miniature staircase model and reached to the rear of her chair for her portable toolbox to begin putting it together.

Ms. Parkly hovered nearby. "Can I help?"

"Don't touch that," Ridley said, shifting a chisel away from her teacher's accident-prone hands. She then picked up a fine-pointed screwdriver to attach some small cogs to the model's rubber bands. "Maybe you could go find me a cup of water," she suggested without looking up.

"Will you be all right by yourself?"

That made Ridley look up. "Of course I'll be fine by myself." She couldn't stop her face from twisting into a sneer.

"Ah. Well. Then I'll be back in a jiff." Ms. Parkly walked away quickly.

Replaying her words in her head, Ridley felt suddenly guilty. She'd have to spend the entire train ride back to Mineral Wells doing magic tricks to smooth things over. She had let her quick temper (and her nerves) take over once again.

Across the aisle, a group of young participants was setting up their own table. They were working together to arrange something they'd named THE GARDEN OF THE FUTURE. They had a lush green diorama filled with miniature plants and trees. Each member of the group unveiled a special tool and propped it against the table.

One looked like a modified hand trowel with some sort of electric panel stuck to the short shaft. Another was a divot-making device—its head a toothy, spinning mechanism that looked like it could punch out pieces of earth. A third looked like an ordinary shovel...until a member of the group flipped a switch and it began vibrating. Perhaps to help a digger get through hard-packed earth.

The group laughed at something, and Ridley was struck with a memory of her own friends—her magicians club. She was suddenly jealous of the young inventors who had one another for support and warmth and chatter, when all she had was a klutzy, overly enthusiastic teacher. For the first time that morning, Ridley wished Theo, Leila, Carter, and the twins could be here with her, to cheer her on.

(And who wouldn't? Even after the friends' recent, shall we say, bumps in the road, I assure you that the Misfits were wishing they could be with Ridley to cheer her on too.)

Someone at the corner of her vision was staring. Ridley looked down the long aisle to find an older woman standing with her shoulders slumped, her arms hanging limply, her lips parted slightly as if she was about to speak but had forgotten what she'd wanted to say. Her gray hair was short and curled, and she wore cat-eye glasses and a purple-and-pink-polka-dotted dress. After a moment, Ridley recognized her: It was Mrs. Maloney, a librarian in Mineral Wells. She'd also been one of the judges of the talent show at the end of the summer.

Mrs. Maloney shivered, her head twitching slightly. She started toward Ridley. Her lips were moving, but Ridley couldn't make out what she was saying. Her steps were deliberate, one foot before the other, so that her hips swayed back and forth, back and forth, hypnotically.

The librarian grabbed the shovel from the table across from Ridley's project, then slowly turned around.

"What are you doing?" Ridley asked sharply. "Put that down!"

The woman's glassy eyes bulged, bloodshot and watery, full of fear and also...*determination*?

Ridley could finally hear what she was whispering to herself. It sent chills across her scalp.

"What have I done? What have I *done*?"

The librarian raised the shovel. Ridley flipped a trigger in the arm of her chair.

"What have I done?"

Ridley's wheels spun, and she shot backward, just as Mrs. Maloney lumbered toward the table holding her staircase project.

"Stop!" Ridley shouted, seeing what was about to happen. "Nooooo!"

The woman swung the shovel down. Ridley's wooden model splintered.

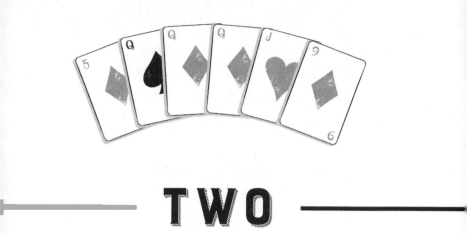

TWO

Mrs. Maloney slammed the shovel down again. Cog works, springs, and gears crumpled.

Ridley held up her hands as pieces of her project exploded outward, hitting her like shrapnel from a bomb.

All around, people turned to see what was happening. A hubbub rose up as the young inventors and their patrons shouted and scattered.

The night of the talent show appeared in Ridley's mind, the events playing out simultaneously as the librarian continued to whack away at the remnants of her model.

Wham!

The magic shop's windows exploded outward in a sparkling flash.

Wham!

The walls crumbled. Dust enveloped Main Street.

Wham!

Carter, Leila, and Theo took off toward the shop, leaving Ridley in the park with Emily Meridian, the Golden twins, and the animals.

Wham!

The mesmerist appeared from the shadows, surrounded by smoke, his collar pulled high, obscuring his face.

Kalagan...

The man who had terrorized Ridley and her friends since the beginning of the summer, who had placed the dynamite in the bootlegger tunnels below Vernon's Magic Shop, who had flipped the switch, who had changed everything.

The woman was yelling now. *"What have I done? What have I done?"* But her voice sounded robotic, like an empty mantra, or a chorus to a nonsensical song.

Those were the words that Kalagan had said on the night of the blast, just before he'd come after Theo with the magic wand that had turned into a blade.

The librarian finally dropped the shovel and began to wrestle with Ridley's poster.

Ridley saw red. How dare this woman ruin her hard work? And worse: How dare she invoke the man who had been haunting Ridley's dreams? Was she working for him?

Ridley flipped the switch on the arm of her chair again. This time, the chair flew forward. Its footrests slammed into the librarian's shins. Mrs. Maloney cried out, dropping the poster board and falling backward, landing hard on the tile floor. She let out a bleat when she glanced up at Ridley, whose finger was ready to hit the trigger again.

But Ridley could see now that something had changed in the woman's eyes. Mrs. Maloney winced and then rubbed at the spot on her leg where Ridley had smashed her. She looked horrified at the mess she'd made. Releasing a harsh gasp, she said to herself, more softly this time, "What have I done?"

"Ridley!" Ms. Parkly was racing up the aisle, carrying two paper cups. "What's going on?" She tripped as she got close, and ice water flew from the cups, instantly soaking the librarian and sending her into a rigid shock.

Ridley pressed her spine against the back of her chair and glanced around, as if someone else might suddenly lunge at her, but then Ms. Parkly placed herself squarely between Ridley and the woman on the floor.

People in stiff blue uniforms approached. From the patches on their shoulders, Ridley knew they were security guards. One stopped next to Mrs. Maloney, one by Ms. Parkly. Another approached Ridley. When the guard touched her arm, she yelped.

"Are you all right?" he asked. Ridley took in the ruins of her project—all the work, all the anticipation, all the imagination—and felt like she was looking at the inside of her mind.

"No. No, I don't think I am," she admitted.

The security guards led Mrs. Maloney away, but not before she reached out to Ridley, her voice wobbly with emotion. "I don't know what came over me. Please. I didn't mean to—"

But Ms. Parkly stepped forward and said, "And while I didn't mean to dump water all over you, ma'am, I'm not sorry I did!"

Ridley almost laughed. Her teacher's clumsiness had been an asset, for once.

A woman with an immense beehive updo and a man whose glasses had black frames as thick as licorice whips approached and introduced themselves as the administrators of the inventors' fair. Ridley tried her best to explain the situation, Ms. Parkly standing quietly behind her.

"I'm so very sorry this happened, Miss Larsen," said the woman. "We'll investigate the incident alongside the authorities. Is your project salvageable?"

Ridley shook her head.

"It looked very impressive," the woman offered gently.

"Perhaps we could extend an invitation for you to compete next year?" the man added.

Ridley nodded, simply too tired to speak.

Mrs. Maloney had accomplished what she'd set out to do. *Or*, Ridley thought, *she accomplished what someone had wanted her to do*. Her final words echoed in Ridley's memory: *I don't know what came over me. Please. I didn't mean to…*

If the librarian hadn't meant to, then *who* had?

Ridley barely had to consider.

Kalagan was a mesmerist. He must have hypnotized the librarian.

The man was a maniac, and Ridley now knew that the Magic Misfits should never have disbanded to appease him, as Mr. Vernon had instructed. They should have stayed out in the open, just like Ridley wanted to, ready for a fight. But had anyone listened to her?

No.

Hiding in the shadows hadn't made a bit of difference.

★ ★ ★

Back on the train, Ridley tried to force her mind elsewhere, to think about the adjustments she and her father would make to improve her project for next year. When he got back from his sales trip, of course.

Her mother wouldn't like that, Ridley thought, *the two of them spending even more hours tinkering together.* Mrs. Larsen refused to understand her daughter's love of invention. It didn't help that she was usually busy and distracted with her own work, always in the middle of writing another novel filled with romance and intrigue. Sometimes Ridley wondered if her mother wrote them as an escape from a life that she saw as ordinary.

Or worse, annoying.

Pushing thoughts of her mother from her mind, Ridley reached into the panel in her chair and removed her notebook and pen. She needed to write down the details of her encounter with the librarian to share with her friends, to let them know that they all might be in danger.

Again.

Glancing up, she saw Ms. Parkly turn quickly around and slouch in her seat, as if trying to become invisible.

Hmmm... Mrs. Maloney had claimed she hadn't known

what she was doing, and she did appear to have been in a trance. Where had Ms. Parkly been prior to the librarian's shovel attack? She'd been getting Ridley a glass of water. Or so she'd said. Was it possible that her teacher had the same skill as Kalagan? Mesmerism?

"Ms. Parkly?" Ridley said, making her voice as sweet as she could.

"Oh! Yes?" her teacher answered without turning.

"Do you know anything about mesmerism?" Ridley zeroed in on her teacher's scalp, watching for a twitch.

But Ms. Parkly didn't move. "I don't think so," she answered. "Is that something you'd like to learn about this week? What made you think of it?"

Ridley tried to keep her voice sounding chirpy and innocent when she answered. "Oh, nothing. Never mind. Now, how about I show you another magic trick?"

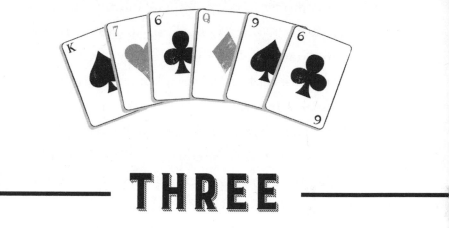

THREE

The train reached Mineral Wells by early afternoon.

Ridley's mom was waiting for them, parked at the curb in front of the station. After such an early morning, it felt to Ridley like the day was nearly done, even though the sun still hung high in the sky. When she was situated in the back seat, her mom peered at her through the rearview mirror and said, "You made it back in one piece!"

"My project didn't."

Mrs. Larsen blinked. "Well, that's obvious, Ridley.... I mean, your teacher told me...and of course it's awful...but maybe now you'll spend a little more time on what you're *supposed* to be doing together and—my gosh, *look at the time*! I've got to get to town. We have absolutely nothing for dinner at home....I can't write on an empty stomach."

Ridley rolled her eyes as they sped away from the station. It was just like her mother to dismiss what had happened and get back to doing what she did best: Worry about Ridley's schoolwork. Worry about dinner. Worry about deadlines.

To Ridley's surprise, Ms. Parkly piped up. "Ridley did a swell job of protecting herself, Mrs. Larsen." Ridley felt a surge of pride, but then quickly remembered that Ms. Parkly was now on her *suspicious* list. When her teacher turned to give her a small smile, Ridley scowled.

After dropping off Ms. Parkly at her apartment near the mill, Ridley asked her mother if she could come to town with her.

"Well...all right...but we can't dawdle....I've got to get back to work....The words were flowing so well this morning before I had to come get you at the station.... I've really got to—goodness, *watch where you're going*!" she shrieked as another car inched a bit too close to theirs.

"We're barely moving, Mom," Ridley said grumpily. What she didn't share was that she'd already made plans for that afternoon in the village and wouldn't be returning home with her mother.

It had been over a week since the Magic Misfits had seen one another, and that hadn't even been an official meeting. They'd gathered in the back room of the Tip Top Bowling Arcade to play spades, which was only slightly fun, because Carter made the cards disappear one by one, and everyone besides Ridley kept laughing, which of course made Ridley so cross she snapped and then forced herself to apologize.

Ridley felt like she'd been doing a lot of that lately. Snapping. Apologizing. She'd watched her mother and father relate to each other this way ever since she could remember. She wondered sometimes if it was why her father spent so much time on the road.

"Ridley?"

Ridley jolted. "Huh?"

Mrs. Larsen pulled the car into a space on the street. "You're not listening to me."

"Yes, I am. I just..." Ridley felt her cheeks warm. "Say it again?"

Mrs. Larsen let out a huff. "I wanted to know if you

were going to…not that I'm necessarily advocating that you do….Oh dear, we really do need to hurry….What was I just saying? Oh, I was asking if you were going to rebuild your project. The one that got broken today."

Ridley almost thought she sensed a hidden meaning in her mother's question. Something like: *Are you okay?*

Why couldn't anyone in this family just say what they meant, Ridley wondered, *instead of hiding it underneath layers of riddles and disguise?*

"I think so…but now that the inventors' fair is over, I don't really see the point."

"I suppose I have to agree with you," Mrs. Larsen replied. "All right. Let's go, then."

In the village, Ridley trailed her mother, who walked in the direct center of the sidewalk. Ridley was sure she was in too much of a hurry to realize she was taking up the entire space. Ridley's chair rolled over fallen leaves, red and yellow, though most of the trees lining the street were still green.

Tourists were out in full force. Visitors loved coming to the picturesque town on weekends this time of year—photographing the foliage, hiking the hills, picking apples and pumpkins and gourds at local farms. This was the last hurrah before the coming

winter. Ridley didn't like the chillier seasons. It was difficult to navigate slush after snowfall, and often the brisk air left her with a prickly discomfort deep in her muscles. She would bring it up to her father when he came home again; maybe there was a modification they could make to the tires of her chair so they wouldn't slide on ice. Deeper treads maybe? Or a grittier rubber? Or maybe electric heaters attached to the bottoms of the footrests.

Mrs. Larsen opened the door to the cheese shop, and Ridley followed her inside. It was a skinny space, and it was crowded. Mrs. Larsen let out a moan when she saw the number of people waiting to be helped.

Ridley moved to the back of the shop and amused herself by rearranging the shelves of preserves and honey beside her. One woman approached a canister of mashed figs and reached to pick it up, but when she held it in her hands the canister appeared to turn into a fig-shaped rock. The woman let out a surprised "Wha—?" as Ridley turned away, laughing to herself. Ridley knew Mr. Vernon said that doing magic was supposed to make people smile, but sometimes watching them jump in surprise was just as satisfying.

And speaking of jumping in surprise, Ridley felt her chest clench as she heard a raised voice come from the front of the store, near the register. Peering across the space, Ridley saw her mother arguing with the cheesemonger (which, in case you were about to giggle, is the *actual* title of someone who sells cheese).

Mrs. Larsen shouted, "Wouldn't you think it a courtesy to phone your customer if they were expecting a delivery that had not arrived?"

The cheesemonger, a youngish woman with a mouse-brown ponytail pulled up into a net, choked out an apology. But Ridley's mother wouldn't let up.

"Next time, I'll be taking my cheese-business to Murray's mail order, thank you very much." Ridley didn't believe that her mother ever actually had very much *cheese-business* (I, on the other hand, delight in my weekly order of Gouda, Taleggio, and Camembert), but still, it was embarrassing. What was even more embarrassing was when Mrs. Larsen called to the back of the store. "Come on, Ridley! We have to get to the greengrocers before they run out of brussels sprouts...or was I going to make asparagus? Maybe it was broccoli? Oh, I'm all muddled now....*Ridley!* Oh, there you are....Let's get moving. Without my cheese, I have to completely rethink dinner." Ridley wanted to shrink into the floor as she made her way through the crowd.

As she passed the cheesemonger (*stop giggling!*), she overheard a customer say in a low voice (but not *too* low), "Bless that woman's heart. Has to do everything on her own with that husband of hers on the road again. If I had as much on my plate as she does, I'd be yelling at everyone all the time too."

Ridley frowned. What a bunch of busybodies. She veered the arm of her chair into the customer's rear end. When they startled and hopped out of the way, Ridley called out, "Excuse *you!* Some of us have better things to do than gossip the day away!"

By the time she'd made it out to the sidewalk, she regretted saying anything at all. People were looking at her the same way they'd stared at her mother.

After following her mom to the greengrocer and listening to her mutter angrily, Ridley checked her watch. "Is it all right if I go get some air?"

"What's wrong with *this* air?" asked Mrs. Larsen.

"I just...need some time to think," said Ridley.

"Fine...but be home before dark....Wait—did we pass the grocer already? How did I miss it? I could have sworn...Ridley! Be home before dark, I said, and...keep an eye out for crazed librarians, please!" Her mother gave a half wave as she bustled back the way they'd come.

Ridley wasn't sure if that last bit was meant to be a joke or an actual warning. Either way, it chafed as she made her way to the agreed-upon meeting place. The Orpheum Theater had been closed for as long as she could remember. The marquee over the formerly grand front entry was lined with light bulbs that hadn't glowed in years, and the letters that spelled out titles of old films were crooked and looked about ready to crash down to the sidewalk below. Next to the newspaper-covered front door, an alleyway reached toward the back of the building. It was barely wide enough for Ridley's chair.

Glancing around to make sure no one was watching, she entered the shadows, a chill emanating from the brick walls on either side. At the end of the passage, there was a slight ramp up to a door that was propped open with a broken brick.

Ridley used her door-opening device to open it farther. The space was dark, the air filled with musty dampness. She pushed a button near the top of her right wheel, and a small light illuminated the way forward. As Ridley continued into the shadows, the rear of the giant screen rose up before her, a white panel that was a couple of stories tall. Just behind it, several empty chairs were arranged in a circle—Leila's doing from the last time the Misfits had met here. "Hello?" Ridley called, making her voice stern. "Anyone there?"

An eerie silence answered her. Something didn't feel right.

A sputtering of clicks was followed by a burst of illumination upon the rear of the movie screen.

"Surprise!"

Ridley's friends dashed out from the shadows, each holding a flashlight. She pressed her hand to her mouth, her heart locomoting inside her rib cage. Carter, Leila, Theo, Olly, and Izzy cheered until Ridley couldn't help but reveal her grin. "Misfits!" she yelled. "It's not a *surprise* if we've already planned to meet."

"Oh, shush," said Leila, the buttons on her jacket jingling like bells. Her smile was wide, her brown eyes beaming. "We've been planning for this for a week." The other Misfits stepped aside and shone their lights upon Leila as she bounded into the circle of chairs. "Ridley Larsen! Congratulations on your victorious return to Mineral Wells!"

Theo held his light under his head. He did not dress in his trademark tuxedo any longer. Since the Misfits were supposed to have disbanded, he'd decided to make his look less formal, less like a performer. Today he wore high-waisted beige slacks and a black turtleneck sweater. "Everyone knew you would do well at the fair," he said, "and since our magic club is together again, the rest of us have prepared a show in your honor!"

The others clapped and cheered, and Ridley felt her face start to warm. "But I—"

"Shh!" said Carter, winking. He wore a brown corduroy coat, and even in the dim room, his blond hair

practically shone and his blue eyes twinkled.

Ridley rubbed at her temples. Her friends had done something nice for her. Couldn't she just enjoy it?

Inside the circle, Leila brought an intricately knotted net from behind her back and laid it on the ground. Stepping into its center, she gathered up the corners over her head. "Olly! Izzy! Your assistance, please."

The twins cartwheeled between the chairs. They tied the top of Leila's net tightly, so that it appeared as though she had been captured in a forest trap. "Oh no! Whatever shall I do?" Leila crooned from inside the net.

Ridley let herself chuckle.

Olly and Izzy then brought out an enormous pink silk kerchief and held it before Leila like a curtain. Hidden, she shouted out, "One...Two..." On "Three!" the twins dropped the silk to reveal that the intricately knotted net containing Leila had transformed. Now she was no longer caught inside but was tied up from neck to ankles in the same white rope instead.

"Oops!" Leila cried out.

Ridley let out a loud chortle.

But all was not lost! Leila bent at the waist, rolled forward, and by the time she stood up again, the rope had loosened, falling to the ground in a neat coil. Leila stepped over it and took a bow as the others applauded loudly.

Ridley fully gave in and let out a whoop.

(Doesn't it feel nice to let yourself be caught up sometimes? I try to *whoop* at least three times a day myself.)

Leila leapfrogged over the back of a chair as Theo took her place inside the ring. The twins stayed where they were, raising the piece of pink silk between them again. Theo stood before it and began, "As you know, I have spent much time dedicated to the art of levitation. Almost as much time as I've spent dedicated to playing my music!" He moved his arm from his side, and his violin appeared in his hand. He twirled the violin, and his bow appeared in the other. "In this trick, I shall combine the two arts and make them more than they could ever be on their own." He raised the violin to his chin and began to play. The tune started off slow and quiet, and as Theo continued, he walked around the cloth curtain that Olly and Izzy were holding up for him. His music bounced around the old movie theater, growing louder, the melody moving quickly.

To Ridley's surprise, Theo's head appeared at the top of the silk cloth. His eyes were closed, and he fluttered his bow across the strings as if the tune itself were lifting him up and up and up. Soon, his entire body was revealed, as if he were floating over the space behind the pink cloth. He opened his eyes and looked down at the twins. They took that as their cue to lower the cloth slowly down—so too came Theo, playing all the while. When the top hem of the cloth was a foot off the ground, Theo stepped forward, his feet landing firmly on the floor. With a final trill, he bowed quickly as the twins whipped the cloth aside, revealing the nothingness that had been holding Theo aloft.

The trick was too good for Ridley to not honk the horn hidden under the seat of her chair. Theo grinned back at her.

Carter stepped forward. He placed one hand behind his back. Raising the other over his head, he snapped his fingers. When he brought the first hand out again, a small cake was balanced on his palm, a single sparkler spitting glints and gleams into the darkness.

Ridley's eyes began to sting with emotion.

"Congratulations, Ridley!" Carter said.

"Congratulations, Ridley!" the other Misfits echoed.

The sparkler fizzled out. In the sudden dark, Ridley wiped at her cheeks. "I—I don't know what to say."

Carter handed the cake to Theo.

"You don't have to say anything," Leila answered.

Theo mussed Ridley's curls. "I mean, you *could* say thank you."

"And that's not all," Carter added mysteriously. With a flourish, he was holding one of Mr. Vernon's top hats—one that had survived the destruction at the magic shop. He tilted it toward her, revealing that it was empty. Even though Ridley knew what was coming, she felt a thrill. Carter held the hat upright, reached inside, and then pulled out a fluffy white rabbit. The animal scrunched up its nose at Ridley.

"My Top Hat!" Ridley clapped, taking her pet into her arms.

"He's been a very good boy at our new suite up at the resort," said Leila.

"Top Hat is *always* a good boy," Ridley replied. She kissed the rabbit's forehead. "Aren't you just?"

"Olly's a good boy too," said Izzy, appearing on one side of Ridley.

"And Izzy's a good girl," said Olly, showing his freckled face at the other side.

"Yes, but the real question is: Can *you* disappear inside a magician's hat?" Leila asked with a grin.

Olly and Izzy gawped at each other. "Why didn't we think of that before?" cried Olly. "We'll have to try it!" said Izzy. Together, the twins plopped down onto two seats beside Ridley, shaking their purple coats from their shoulders. Izzy shook so hard, she fell to the floor—an obvious pratfall that sometimes grated Ridley's nerves, but today she welcomed the silliness.

(The world will always need silliness, my friends.)

"How's Mr. Vernon?" Ridley asked. "And the Other Mr. Vernon?"

"Everyone is doing well," said Leila. "My dad keeps saying, '*Hope springs eternal.*' I'm not sure if it's another of his secret messages to us, or if it's just another of his philosophies. Either way, I'm sure they would both wish you a fond hello, if they knew that we were meeting today."

Carter raised an eyebrow, then whispered, "I'm pretty sure they know we're meeting today. They always seem to know."

Ridley's stomach lurched as the reality of the Misfits' situation came crashing back down on her. As happy as the last few moments with her friends had felt, she had to tell them what had happened earlier in the day. She cleared her throat. "I didn't win the inventors' fair."

"So what?" said Leila. "We're still proud of you!"

"You don't understand," Ridley answered. "Something bad happened this morning. Something that has to do with *all of us*. I think that K—"

"Do not say it," Theo whispered, as if to himself.

But Ridley *had* to say it. She held back a shudder.

"I think Kalagan is back."

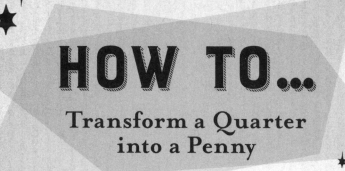

HOW TO...

Transform a Quarter into a Penny

I know...*I know!* What an inopportune time to be teaching you a new magical skill. That said, I find I always appreciate a diversion after the name *Kalagan* is uttered. Let's put him out of our minds for a few moments and learn a trick that Ridley would particularly enjoy: how to transform one kind of coin into another—right in the palm of your hand!

WHAT YOU'LL NEED:

A silver quarter or large coin

A copper penny or a small coin of a different color

A piece of double-sided tape

A tabletop

TO PREPARE:

Stick a small piece of double-sided tape to the palm of your right hand. (Make sure you don't wave or shake hands with anyone and accidentally reveal the tape.)

STEPS:

1. Present the quarter to your audience in the palm of your left hand, while also quickly showing them that you have nothing in your right.

SECRET MAGIC MOVE:

The penny should be completely hidden underneath the quarter.

2. Wave your right hand slowly over the coins. Wiggle your fingers and say something magical.

3. Bring your right hand down so that the double-sided tape sticks to the quarter.

4. Lift your right hand with the quarter now stuck to it, revealing the penny in your left palm. (While looking at the penny, flick the quarter off your right hand and into your lap—somewhere it won't make noise when it lands!)

5. Hold up the penny for your audience to admire. Look as surprised as they are.

6. Take a bow!

FOUR

"*Kalagan?*" Olly blurted out.

Ridley nodded.

"I'm getting really sick of that guy," Izzy muttered.

(Friends, so am I. *So. Am. I.*)

"What happened at the fair?" asked Carter.

"Everyone take a seat, and I'll tell you." The others pulled chairs close. As Ridley spoke, she felt like she was sharing a scary tale. She leaned forward, the glow from the flashlights beaming up from below. They all listened in horror as Ridley described how Mrs. Maloney had destroyed her invention.

"That's so awful!" said Leila.

"Were you hurt?" asked Theo.

Olly and Izzy put their hands on her chair, as if that might comfort her.

"I wasn't hurt," said Ridley. "But that shovel was sharp. And if Mrs. Maloney had decided to swing it at me..." She shivered at the thought. "The scariest part was what she said afterward. That she didn't know what she was doing...It was like...she'd been mesmerized."

The others grew still.

"And who do we know with that skill?" Ridley went on.

"I don't want to hear his name anymore," said Leila. "You think...*he* mesmerized the librarian to come after you?"

Ridley nodded. "Kalagan or...someone else."

"Any idea who?" asked Theo.

"My teacher. Ms. Parkly."

"Miss *Sparkly*?" Olly asked. "That's a funny name."

"Parkly," Ridley repeated. "No *S*."

"I thought you liked her," said Carter.

"I never said that. And even if I didn't...you know...*dislike* her at first, she could still be another one of Kalagan's goons. She showed up in town right after the explosion at the magic shop, and we know we can't trust people who randomly appear in Mineral Wells."

"Not necessarily," said Theo. "When your dad left for his trip, your mom needed someone to take over his teaching duties. Could it be a coincidence?"

Ridley nodded. "Someone might have wanted it to *look* like one."

Leila gasped and then stood.

"What's wrong?" asked Carter, glancing around the dim space. "Did you hear something?"

"No," she answered. "It's just...Remember a couple days ago when we were at the grocery store with Poppa?" A light went on in Carter's face, and his jaw opened slowly. Leila turned to the others. "We'd filled a couple baskets with ingredients for a new pie that Poppa wanted to make, and when we got to the register, Bradley, the cashier, looked...*funny*. His eyes were glassy, as if they were seeing something far away. He was whispering something."

Carter went white as a sheet. *"What have I done?"*

"That's what the librarian said just before she attacked me!" said Ridley.

Leila nodded quickly. The buttons on her jacket

jingled as she shivered. "Then he dumped every ingredient from our baskets onto the floor!"

"Rude!" said Olly.

Carter huffed. "Afterward, Bradley looked up at the Other Mr. Vernon and smiled. He said, 'Can I help you?' as if we'd approached him empty-handed. We had to point out the mess he'd made!"

"Bradley apologized over and over," said Leila. "And he helped us gather up new ingredients. Do you think someone hypnotized him too?"

Ridley drummed her fingers on the wheels of her chair. "Kalagan said that the night of the explosion. *'I'm Dante Vernon. What have I done?'* I think...I think he knows we're still meeting."

Theo cleared his throat. "Something similar happened last weekend when my parents took me to see a symphony at that converted barn space outside of town. One of the ushers...He was whispering something I could not make out, an odd look on his face. He approached us and then just...fell into me. Nearly knocked me out of my seat. I thought he had simply tripped. But now..."

Izzy reached across Ridley and smacked Olly in the arm. "Ow!" he cried out, but then Izzy shushed him, a look of seriousness knitted in her brow. "We had a heckler during one of our shows in the resort's lobby this week."

"Oh *yeah*," said Olly, remembering.

"Or we *thought* he was a heckler. He was sorta acting like what you all experienced. Muttering something weird. It could have been, '*What have I done?*' Right, Olly?"

"Left," Olly answered. "I mean…*Correct*. And then he started singing along with us, but he didn't know the lyrics. And the ones he made up…Let's just say, if *we* sang them, we'd have been fired."

"Fired and grounded," Izzy whispered. "Our parents got us out of there pretty quickly. And afterward, when they demanded an apology, Mr. Arnold said that the guest couldn't remember messing with us and so he refused."

Ridley nodded. "Kalagan is up to something rotten."

"What's with these attacks?" asked Leila, hugging her torso. "What does he *want*? He's already taken everything from us. We can't do magic together. We can barely *be* together."

(Oh, Leila. How I wish I could tell her that this is

exactly what Kalagan desires—to keep those who work against him apart. To make them feel helpless and alone. And yet, the Misfits still have one another. Just as you have me, dear reader. And I you.)

"He likes making chaos," said Theo. "He must think it is fun."

"Ooh, ooh, you know what's *actually* fun?" Olly asked. When no one answered, he replied in a small voice, "Trampolines." When Izzy raised an eyebrow, he added, "But they *are* fun."

"Back to the topic at hand," Ridley went on. "What are we going to do about it?"

"About trampolines?" Izzy asked.

"About Kalagan's return!" Ridley said, trying to control her voice. "About the attacks. About...*us*. Hiding in the shadows. Pretending that we're no longer friends."

"Is that not what Mr. Vernon wants us to do?" asked Theo.

Ridley shrugged, raising her shoulders in exaggeration. "Look at what's happening," she said. "Each of us has encountered someone who's been mesmerized. Someone who has tried to hurt us. Or embarrass us. Or scare us."

"What are you suggesting?" asked Leila.

"To quote Madame Helga: '*Alone we are weak. Together we are strong.*'" Ridley steadied her jaw. "It's time to bring the Magic Misfits back."

FIVE

"We come out from underground," Ridley went on. "Show Kalagan that he can't intimidate us." Each of the Magic Misfits glanced around the circle, as if waiting for someone to answer Ridley. "Well?" She looked at them expectantly. "What do you say?"

"Maybe we shouldn't," Leila said softly. "My dad gave us instructions to keep us safe. We already know Kalagan is violent. How much further will he go to prove his point?"

"Which is?" asked Ridley.

"That he hates Dante," Carter suggested. "That he

blames him for the deaths of his parents. It's a pretty serious threat, Ridley. I'm with Leila. I say we leave this to the Vernons to figure out."

"*We* are the ones who keep thwarting him," said Theo. Carter scowled. "Do not misunderstand me, Carter. I agree with both you and Leila. The Vernons know what they are doing, but the Magic Misfits are still the ones being targeted. Kalagan has wanted the names of Mr. Vernon's Magic Circle for a long time now. He wants Vernon's friends to join his criminal enterprise so that he can use all of their magical skills to help him line his pockets. I can only imagine that he is sending these mesmerized people after us as another threat. Not only to Mr. Vernon, but also to *us*. He wants to make sure we leave him alone. It is likely he knows that we never actually disbanded. I think the Misfits should try to sit down again with Mr. Vernon. Talk this out. He should know what is going on."

Ridley shook her head. "What if we tell Mr. Vernon about all of this, and he still wants us to stay apart?" She took a deep breath, hoping that her friends couldn't see her trembling. She wasn't quite ready to share how much she had missed them, that she wanted them to come together to stop Kalagan once and for all, but *also* just to be together again. And if that took break-ing some rules...She steamrolled forward. "I think we should *confront* our attackers...Ask them ourselves—"

"I think that is a really bad idea!" Theo exclaimed.

Ridley felt her skin start to cook. "And *I* think it could work!"

Everyone was silent.

"I think therefore I am?" said Izzy after a moment.

"I am not much of a thinker," said Olly.

Ridley lowered her voice, carefully releasing each word so she wouldn't hurt anyone's feelings. "What do you two *think* about the Magic Misfits meeting in pub-lic again? What do you *think* about the possibility that Kalagan is going around town mesmerizing people so that they'll hurt us?"

"Honestly, I'm not sure," said Izzy, coming down to earth. "I guess I don't really understand how Kala-gan is doing what he's doing. Is he like actually magi-cally mystical?"

"I wonder the same thing," said Olly. "Shouldn't we look into it?"

"Yes!" said Ridley, revealing her notebook. "An actual good idea, you two. Bravo, Olly. Bravo, Izzy." The twins stood and gave a slight bow. "Thankfully,

I've already done that research! And I have my notes. Right here."

Theo sighed. "Go on, then. Tell us what you know."

"I found some great sources on the concept of mesmerism," Ridley began. "Throughout history, it's been used for many purposes—some practical, others...not. In ancient cultures, hypnosis was used as a method of healing. Priests, shamans, and other spiritual leaders would chant and pray over their followers and put them to sleep, or they'd do a ritual they believed would influence and improve the mind of someone who was sick." She flipped through some pages. "Over a century ago, a doctor named Franz Mesmer invented a scientific procedure to investigate his patients' minds. He'd put them into a trance, get them to look into their memories, and then suggest changes to their behavior. When the patient woke from the trance, they had no memory of talking with the doctor."

"*What have I done?*" Carter murmured.

Ridley nodded. "This procedure became known as *mesmerism*. More recently, entertainers latched onto the idea. Some performers have even used mesmerism to frighten people. A common thread I discovered was that when performed onstage, the act is easily faked."

"*Faked*, like Sandra Santos's psychic act?" Leila asked.

"And B. B. Bosso's sideshow performers!" Theo suggested.

"Exactly. What we need to find out is how *real* are Kalagan's powers? Is he like the shamans of old? Is he like Dr. Mesmer? If Kalagan *is* getting inside the heads of Mineral Wells citizens, then we need to figure out how to help them get out from under his grip."

"Or maybe he is just a charlatan," said Theo. "A con artist."

"Like my uncle Sly!" said Carter.

Ridley nodded again. "If he *is* just a con artist, then Kalagan has still somehow found a way to get people to do his bidding. Which would make it easier for us to stop him, because it removes any mystical element from his attacks."

"I don't believe in mysticism," said Carter.

Leila chimed in. "I don't know. I like to imagine that magic exists on some level. Real magic. Not just tricks."

"Whatever the case," Ridley went on, "I thought it would be helpful for us to know as much about our opponent as possible, so I took it upon myself to look up Kalagan's history. Since the end of the summer,

I've visited the town hall, the records office, and some local newspapers. I would have just gone to Mr. Vernon himself, but as we all know, he keeps secrets."

"Only when he's trying to protect us," Leila said.

"What else have you got in your notebook?" Carter asked.

"This Kalagan fella has lived quite a life," said Ridley, riffling through more pages. "Let's see. Kilroy Kalagan was born a little over four decades ago, right here in Mineral Wells to a young couple named Augustus and Diana."

"Kilroy?" Theo repeated, shuddering. "His name is *Kilroy*?"

Ridley flipped over another page. "Oh, this part was surprising: Kilroy actually had a twin brother named Kincaid."

"Twins!" Olly blurted, reaching across Ridley and smacking his sister's arm. "Just like us."

Izzy made a shocked face. "Hopefully not like us at all!"

"Kilroy's brother, Kincaid, died when they were babies."

"How sad!" Leila cried out.

"That's probably what messed him up," said Theo.

"Some of us have lost family members without turning into criminals," said Carter.

Theo's brown eyes went wide. "I am sorry, Carter. I did not mean—"

Ridley cleared her throat and went on, "Mick Meridian told us about the blaze at the resort, where Kalagan's parents worked. Kilroy and Vernon argued about the Emerald Ring's finale trick for the Mineral Wells talent show. The group was practicing its routines in the basement of the rear lodge when Kilroy's trick sparked a fire. The fire spread quickly to the hotel above them. His parents died as a result, leaving Kilroy an orphan."

"Like me," Carter choked out.

"Not like you." Leila rested her hand on her cousin's shoulder. "Your parents might still be out there."

"Kalagan has since claimed that the fire was Mr. Vernon's fault," Ridley continued. "He blames Vernon for every awful thing in his life."

"Is it weird that I kinda feel bad for him?" asked Leila.

"Yes," said Theo. "But we will try to look past that."

Ridley turned another page. "So, Kilroy ended up at Mother Margaret's Home."

"That's where Dad and Poppa found me!" Leila proclaimed.

"Interesting connection," said Ridley, squinting and making a note in her book. "Kilroy had trouble staying put at the orphanage. He would often take the train back to Mineral Wells, I believe, to check in on the old Emerald Ring. And on Sandra Santos especially, on whom he'd had a crush."

"Creepy," said Theo.

"From there, whenever the authorities dragged Kilroy back to the orphanage, he was always getting into trouble. Stealing the other kids' things. Shoplifting from local stores. And there was one incident that was so disturbing to the staff of the orphanage, they actually had him moved to another home in another part of the state. After that, I couldn't find any more information about him."

"But what was the incident?" asked Olly.

"Yeah!" said Izzy. "You can't just leave that part out."

Ridley sighed. "It's complicated. But from what I could gather from the police report, he tried to make the entire staff of the children's home believe that a burglar was breaking in at night and stealing their valuables. As a precaution, he had them all place their most cherished belongings in a safe. You can probably figure out what happened next."

"He took off with everything?" Carter said, a sneer marking his mouth.

"Bingo!" said Ridley. "One more step on his journey to becoming a full-blown villain."

"But they caught him," said Theo. "He didn't get away with it."

"He was testing his limits," Carter suggested. "Seeing *what* he could get away with. I watched my uncle Sly do the same thing every time we moved to a new town. Asking people for change for a dollar and then switching out the coins until he ended up with at least two more bucks than he'd had. Then there was the cup-game scam. And then there were the flat-out robberies. That was when I decided to take off, because—"

The Misfits spoke in unison: *"You don't steal."*

Leila patted his back. "We know that, Carter."

His face turned pink. "Just sayin'."

Ridley closed her notebook. "So, what do we think? Olly? Izzy? Did any of that help you make a decision?"

"What were we deciding again?" asked Olly.

"We were deciding whether or not to join up with Kalagan, silly!" Izzy answered.

Ridley gritted her teeth. "I seriously hope you're joking."

Izzy smiled. "When am I *not* joking?"

"I think you're right, Ridley," said Olly. "At the very least, we should check in on those people who came after us. See if we can get them to tell us if they've encountered a strange man in a dark cloak and a big top hat."

Ridley's rabbit shifted on her lap and gave a sleepy wheeze, reminding Ridley that he was still with her and available for petting.

"But," said Izzy, "we should do it discreetly. Keep to the shadows. You know? Like Kalagan."

"That's the second most intelligible thing I've heard the two of you say today," Ridley answered. She still sort of thought that her idea of coming out, blasters blaring, would be the best course of action. But after glancing at Theo, Carter, and Leila, she asked, "What do you all think? Do we follow up with our attackers, see if they can point us to where Kalagan is hiding?"

They all nodded tentatively.

"Great," Ridley said with a big nod. "Now...where do we start?"

They agreed to begin tomorrow with the librarian who destroyed Ridley's invention presentation with the garden shovel of the future. Carter and Leila would bring items from the lost and found at the resort for disguises. They'd meet at another of their secret locations—the custodial shed behind the Parks and Recreation Department at the town hall, which was almost always left with the padlock not fully latched. There, they would dress up and make their way to the library a few doors down.

Leaving the room at the back of the old movie theater, the Misfits came out into the alley to find that the sky had already begun to darken. Ridley knew she should head home before her mother started to worry, but she also didn't want to leave her friends just yet. She'd missed them, the squabbling included. She wished they could at least run through a few more tricks, like during a proper meeting. But before she had a chance to mention it, a figure appeared at the end of the alley, blocking their way out.

A low and crinkled voice called out, "Carter Locke? Is that you?"

SIX

A thought shot through Ridley's head: *Kalagan! He's here!*

Carter threw his hands to the sides of his face. "Oh no, oh no, oh no!" He grabbed Leila's wrist, pulling her back toward the theater. The others followed quickly.

"Carter!" The voice came again. "Wait! Don't run!"

Back inside the shadows, Ridley flipped her chair's light on again.

"Who is that man?" Leila whispered, pausing with Carter, who looked dazed.

"My uncle Sly," he answered slowly. "How did he find me?"

"You guys?" Ridley said, trying to mimic Leila's ability to be ever cheery. "Either we need to vanish right now or come up with a plan of attack. Because there's no ramp leading down from this stage to the seating area."

The group was quiet for a moment, listening to harsh footfalls echo closer in the brick alleyway outside.

"We fight," said Carter, whipping two decks of cards from his sleeves and palming them like throwing stars. "Uncle Sly is clever. Hiding will only give us a few seconds to regroup before we have to keep running."

Leila sidled up next to him. She pulled on one of her jangly buttons and a long piece of white magician's rope stretched out of her coat. Leila wrapped the rope around her forearm, catching it between her thumb and around the back of her elbow, as if preparing to make a lasso.

Theo joined the line, slapping his arm against his leg. His violin bow appeared in his hand. The twins flanked the group on either side, fists raised, their faces uncharacteristically serious. At the front of them,

Ridley turned her chair to face the door, feeling like the driver of a tank. She gripped the wheels and steadied herself, taking comfort knowing that her chair was tricked out with all sorts of gadgets she could use to distract, confuse, or vanquish a would-be assailant. She turned off the headlight.

The echoing footfalls slowed as the man came around the corner. A shadow sliced the daylight on the floor. "Carter?" said the man. "I know you're scared. And you have every right to be." His voice was slow. Purposeful. Speaking how you would to a cornered animal you didn't wish to startle. "I've been looking for you for a long time now, boy. I'm not here to hurt you."

The man stepped into the theater. Ridley flashed her light right into his face. "Stop right there," she bellowed.

The man did as he was told, planting his feet on the warped floorboards, blocking the glare from his eyes. His frayed tweed vest hung from a wiry frame.

His greasy, thinning hair looked as if it had been hastily cut without the benefit of a mirror. Stray whiskers poked from his chin. "Carter?" his voice came again, softly. "Who are these kids?"

"Leave us alone," said Theo, holding up his bow like a sword.

"Yeah!" said Izzy. "We know gymnastics!"

Olly nodded fiercely. "And we're not afraid to use them!"

"Relax," said the man. "I get it. You're a team. A gang. Good for you, Carter."

"Not one step closer," Ridley warned, "or you'll find out what this *team* can do."

"Listen, boy," the man said with a sigh. "I admit, I have not been the best guardian all these years. I don't blame you for running away at the train yard. I was wrong to try and steal old Ms. Zalewski's necklace. She was your friend and I should have respected that." He clasped his hands before himself, worrying at his dirty skin. "After you left, I did some digging deep in my soul, and I realized that how we were living our lives was hurtful to you. To both of us. As a family. I...I decided to make a change. I joined a church group in town. I made some new friends—just like you did here, apparently. Created a new world for myself. One where you and I can finally settle down, have a home, where I can raise you right, and you can help me remember how to be...well, how to be good." The man took a step toward the Misfits. Ridley gripped her wheels even harder.

Carter managed to answer. "It's not my job to help you be good."

Flustered, Uncle Sly went on, "Well, I know it ain't your job. You've got to go to school and to play with your friends and eat well and know your prayers. This ain't about me, boy. This is about us. I've looked for you a *long* time—"

"I don't care!" Carter yelled, and the man shut his mouth. Ridley watched a flicker of something cross the man's eyes. Discomfort? Sadness? Rage? "I've been running from you for a long time," Carter went on. "I have a new family. A real family and friends here in Mineral Wells. Things that you could never give me. Never understand! Forget you found me and *get out of here.*"

Ridley's skin went to gooseflesh. She'd never heard anyone talk to an adult that way. She wanted to turn around and give Carter a high five, but she didn't want to move the light off his uncle's eyes.

"*Bo-oyy*," said the man, a half growl that somehow turned into a chortle. "I know that's just the hurt and the anger in you. You and your friends follow me out of this alley. We'll go somewhere. Sit and talk. You got a new guardian? Heck, ask them to join us. You'll see I'm not all bad."

"What's wrong with you?" Carter asked. "I said no!"

The man's brow darkened. "I'm not taking *no* for an answer."

"Well then, that's going to be a problem." Carter stamped his foot, and the Magic Misfits straightened their spines, standing as tall as each of them could. Ridley felt Top Hat nuzzle into her stomach, as if he were terrified, so she placed her hand on the rabbit's neck. "Because *that's* my answer," Carter went on. "Leave us alone!"

Carter's uncle Sly tilted his head back and glared down his nose at the group. "That's how it's gonna be?"

"That's…" Carter's voice began to tremble. "That's how it's going to be."

Uncle Sly stared at Carter for a few long seconds. Ridley was unable to read what was going through the man's mind, and it scared her to imagine how good he must be at hiding what was in there. Then, with a sigh, Uncle Sly nodded. He held out his arm to the door. "You're free to leave. I won't stop ya."

"You first, mister," said Ridley.

"As you wish, *kiddos*." And with that, Uncle Sly stepped out the theater's rear exit. But before he swung the door shut again, he called to Carter. "I'll be in town for a few days, boy. Just in case ya change your mind or something. Find me at the boardinghouse on June Street. Just around the corner." He paused, his eyes seeming to water, then added, "I really hope ya do." Then he turned on his heel and closed the door all the way, leaving the Magic Misfits alone in the dark, with only Ridley's light to see by.

SEVEN

"Are you okay, Carter?" Leila asked, grabbing his shoulders and pulling him into a hug.

Carter managed to speak through the squeeze. "Actually, I think I am. I've been worried ever since the beginning of the summer that Sly would come looking for me. It feels like a weird relief knowing it finally happened."

"A relief?" Ridley asked. "Even if he came here to hurt you?"

"Hurt him?" said Theo. "Did you not hear what

the man said? He wants to bring Carter *home* with him. He said he has changed."

"You can't take the word of a man like that!" Ridley felt her voice rising. "People lie, Theo. They lie. All. The. Time. Especially people who want something from you. You should know that more than the rest of us." The face of Emily Meridian flashed in Ridley's memory. Theo's eyes crinkled to angry slits.

"Okay, okay," said Leila, releasing her cousin from her grasp. She held her hands out as if to create a loop that would bring the group together again. "We've just been thrown a curveball. First the Kalagan stuff. And now the return of Carter's uncle." She led them outside, peeking her head into the alley to check for Sly first. "What do we do about it?"

"Continue on as planned," said Ridley. "We meet tomorrow. We talk to the people who attacked us. Press them for information."

"I'm confused," said Izzy.

Olly held his hand to her forehead. "Confused is our middle name, sis."

Izzy shook him off. "If we've decided to not worry about Carter's uncle Sly coming to Mineral Wells, then I guess we shouldn't worry that he's standing at the end of the alleyway, across the street, pretending to not watch us."

The group turned as one. Izzy was right. Sly was across the street from the alleyway, staring into the window of a candle shop. Clearly, he was using its reflection to spy on them.

Carter shuddered, all of his confidence falling away. "What now?" he asked.

"We escape," said Leila.

★ ★ ★

The plan was this: Olly and Izzy, who were the fastest of them, would approach Uncle Sly and distract him with a jazzy tap dance routine, while the others split into pairs and scattered. They'd reconvene at Ridley's house, which was the closest safe spot.

(Oh, dear reader, have you ever made a plan that went quickly awry? Where your best intentions were thwarted before you even had a chance to find out if they might have worked? Well, I'm sorry to say, *this* plan went just like *that*.)

Before the Golden twins made it even halfway across the street, Uncle Sly turned, raising his hands over his head. "Don't come any closer!" he shouted. Olly and

Izzy glanced back at the group. Ridley waved at them to retreat. But before they could, Uncle Sly brought his hands down. Ear-popping sounds exploded at the twins' feet. He'd thrown several Bang Snaps, the kind Mr. Vernon had once kept in boxes at the magic shop. Olly and Izzy jumped out of the way. This gave Sly enough time to focus on the group and see what they were up to.

"Everyone, go!" Carter yelled. "Now!"

The Misfits divided. Olly and Izzy ran directly up the center of the street toward the town hall. Leila and Theo took off in the opposite direction. This left Carter and Ridley to stare down his uncle at the mouth of the theater's alley.

"Climb on," Ridley whispered to Carter as she flicked a switch near her headrest. At the back of the chair, just behind the wheels, two footrests fell down and locked into place.

Carter let out a grunt as he leapt onto the back of the chair. Ridley pushed another button near her lower back, and her wheels spun a moment before catching the ground and shooting the friends up the sidewalk.

"He's coming," Carter said into her ear. Ridley

grabbed at her right wheel, spinning the chair so that it turned into the next alleyway. They flew down it, headed for the open end where they would burst out onto the street parallel to the one they'd entered on.

"He's still on our heels," Carter yelled.

"Isn't there something you can do to slow him down?"

Carter yelped as he realized that he did, indeed, have something. "My cards!"

Ridley heard a soft *zzzzppp* as Carter bent both decks and then let the playing cards whizz back down the alley. Behind them, Uncle Sly yipped. There came the sound of stumbling and bumbling and tripping and falling (which, in case you were wondering, is a pretty satisfying sound when it happens to someone this rotten). As Ridley's chair skidded out onto the sidewalk, she grabbed her left wheel so hard that she spun entirely around. Carter's cards had formed a slick surface on which the soles of Uncle Sly's shiny shoes could not stay put.

"Carter! Wait!" he cried out.

The electric motor whined, and the chair trembled as Ridley released her right wheel and then continued onward. She felt Carter's warmth and weight at her back. "We need a place to hide out," Ridley said over her shoulder.

"There!" Carter pointed to a shop's sign hanging over a doorway a dozen yards ahead.

TOYS.

"Perfect."

Carter hopped off the back of the chair and opened the door. Ridley shoved inside. "We need to get away from the front window in case your uncle's back on his feet."

"Can I help you with something?" asked the saleswoman. The pink walls of the toy shop were lined with glossy white shelves, and the shelves were filled with erector sets, construction kits, boxes with science experiments, jigsaw puzzles, and fashion dolls.

"Just looking!" Ridley practically shouted, flipping the switch that turned off her chair's electric motor.

"We have a private birthday party happening at the rear of the store," said the woman, "so if you could steer clear of—"

"Got it!" Ridley said, aiming her chair exactly toward the spot the woman was warning her about. A crowd of children was gathered around a table loaded with purple frosted cupcakes.

"She told us not to head back there!" Carter whispered worriedly as he followed behind.

"Too bad. I'm saving our hides." Ridley navigated around the children, their faces marked with the violet guts of their party treats.

A few grown-ups glared at her, but a little girl dressed in overalls and a tiara held out a cupcake, proclaiming, "It's my birthday!" Noticing Top Hat nuzzled in Ridley's lap, the girl squealed, "Can I hold the bunny?"

"Maybe later," Ridley murmured, examining the room. The shelves surrounding the party were lined with stuffed animals. Lions. Giraffes. Hippos. Dogs. Cats. Raccoons. Frogs. Penguins. And a few octopuses. Ridley waved at Carter to come closer. "Quick," she said, reaching into a panel at the side of her chair. "Take this. And follow my lead."

After prepping the area, Ridley and Carter moved toward the farthest wall at the back of the shop and waited. The party went on. The two watched the front door. People outside passed by the shop. Each new face that appeared gave Ridley's stomach a jolt.

"Is it safe to head out yet?" Carter asked.

"He's waiting for us," Ridley answered. "Give it a few more minutes."

Less than thirty seconds later, Carter's uncle appeared in the doorway. Sly glanced past the saleswoman as she greeted him, "Can I help—"

"You see two kids come in here?" he asked.

Ridley watched the saleswoman's face as she startled at his gruffness. *Don't do it*, she thought. *Don't*— But then the woman looked toward the back of the store, right at Carter and Ridley. Sly's eyes followed.

"Oh no, oh no, oh no," Carter murmured.

Ridley shushed him as Uncle Sly pushed past the saleswoman. "Hey, kids!" Ridley called out. The young ones all turned to look at her. "You wanna see a magic trick?"

They jumped up and down. "YESSSSS!!!"

Sly shouted over them. "Carter, I'm sorry! I saw your friends sneaking up behind me and I panicked. I was waiting to talk to you again." He squinted as he tried to decide which side of the cupcake table to come around so that he could finally reach them. When he moved to the left, Ridley raised her left hand and shouted, "*Abra-ca-dabra!*" The kids squealed as all of the stuffed animals on that side of the table flew off the shelves and bounced off Carter's uncle. They swarmed to catch the animals, crowding Sly, who was suddenly

trapped in a small sea of screaming children and plush toys.

"Let's go," she whispered to Carter, who dropped the clear fishing line that he'd been holding. If Sly had chosen the right side of the table, Carter was to have pulled on his line, making the animals on the right side fly off the shelves. As it was, now they slipped down the free right side and then rushed out the door.

EIGHT

It was well past dark by the time Ridley and Carter made it to the Larsen house. The rest of the Misfits had gathered on the porch. As Ridley approached the long wooden ramp, she noticed her mother amongst her friends—Ms. Parkly too.

"*Ridley!* My goodness...where were you? I told you to be home *before dark*...and your dinner is cold and ruined...just like that rug you managed to get grease on a few months ago...and I still haven't had time to get it cle— Be careful not to track mud inside my home, young man!" Ridley's mother exclaimed as

Carter stepped toward the door. Taking advantage of the distraction, Ridley made sure to tuck Top Hat under her jacket so her mother wouldn't see, otherwise Mrs. Larsen would start sneezing and then complaining about allergies that may or may not be real.

Carter spoke up. "It's my fault, Mrs. Larsen. My uncle was chasing us. He—"

"It's nobody's fault, Carter," Ridley insisted. "Your uncle is a jerk, that's all."

"He's more than a jerk," Carter whispered.

"Well...yes...everyone inside, I suppose," Mrs. Larsen said, glancing around the quiet neighborhood. "But only until your parents can collect...I mean...I really have to be getting back to work..." She trailed off as she whisked into the kitchen.

The group perched themselves on furniture around the big living room.

"I already called my dads," said Leila. "They should be here in a few minutes."

"And the police are on their way," said Theo.

"The police?" Carter echoed, a scared look on his face.

"They need to know what happened," said Leila. "They can take our statements. Maybe even question your uncle at the boardinghouse where he said he's staying."

"What are you doing here, Ms. Parkly?" Ridley asked.

The teacher jumped at being addressed, and narrowly avoided knocking over a side table lamp as she moved awkwardly across the room to sit next to Ridley. "I was out for a brisk walk, a jaunt, a little tour of the neighborhood, and I thought I might check in on you after what happened at the inventors' fair."

Ridley sighed and practically blew a raspberry in her teacher's face. She gestured to the room. "As you can see, everything is going *just fine*."

Ms. Parkly let out her odd, high-pitched giggle. "Looks like it!"

Ridley rolled her eyes at the Misfits.

"Who wants tea?" Mrs. Larsen asked abruptly, poking her head out. Before anyone had a chance to answer, she added, "No one? All right, then," and scurried back into the kitchen. Ridley glanced at her friends, none of whom noticed her mother's annoyance at having people in her house. Well, none except Theo, who gave Ridley a knowing look. She gritted her teeth and looked away.

"Anyone want to fill me in on this person who was chasing you?" asked Ms. Parkly.

Ridley watched Carter slump down in the love seat beside Leila. "Carter's parents went missing when he was young," said Ridley. Carter nodded for her to continue. Still, Ridley was careful with her words. She didn't want to let Ms. Parkly know that she was suspicious of her. "His uncle Sly took him in. But Sly wasn't a nice guy."

"He's a con artist," Carter added softly. He spent the next few minutes telling Ms. Parkly his woeful tale.

Ridley felt a scurrying in her belly, then realized Top Hat was scratching to be let out from underneath her jacket. She allowed the rabbit to jump down and stretch his legs.

There was a knock at the door. Ridley wheeled across the room, beating her mother to the door. She checked the hole in the telescoped peephole and then tugged the string on the spring-loaded door opener in the foyer.

Four people stood before her. When she looked at the two men in the middle, she felt a burn at the back of her eyes, and the other two figures faded away. She held out her arms and whispered, "Mr. Vernons."

(Or the *Misters Vernon*, if you'll allow me a slight grammatical correction.)

One of the men bent a knee and brought his arms around her shoulders. His curly white hair tickled her cheek. He smelled of amber and warmth and maybe a little bit of cinnamon. Drawing back and holding her at arm's length, he smiled, his dark, thin mustache stretching across his top lip. "Ridley, my dear, how have you been?"

Ridley pulled herself together. She couldn't have herself bursting into tears at the first sight of her beloved mentor in almost a month. But she also knew she couldn't lie to him. "I've been better," she answered.

The Other Mr. Vernon patted her knee. A sad smile was hidden underneath his trim brown beard. "Oh, sweetheart," he said, rubbing a hand across his shaved head. "We *all* have."

Ridley jerked her head toward the doorway to the living room, where the Magic Misfits were waiting. Ms. Parkly stood in the foyer by the stairs. Dante Vernon rose to his full height and called out to the others, "Ah, friends! So wonderful to see you." Then, looking at Carter, he lowered his voice, "Are you okay?" Mr. Vernon gave him a squeeze and a pat on the back, then reassured him, "If not, you will be. I promise."

Ridley looked to the two figures still standing in the doorway—a man and a woman wearing police uniforms. "Are you Miss Larsen?" asked the female officer.

"I am," said Ridley, as politely as possible.

"Please, come in," her mother added with a sigh. "The more, the merrier."

★ ★ ★

Half an hour later, after they had taken everyone's statements, the officers promised they would warn Uncle Sly that he was not to approach the children again.

"That's not going to help anything," Ridley argued.

Her mother grimaced. "Ridley, let the police do their jobs....This is their area of expertise....Watch out for that loose floorboard, Officer....I've been meaning to call a repairman for weeks....Would you know anyone who might—wait—what was I just saying? Oh yes, Ridley, the police are very busy, I'm sure, and need to get back to work...as do we *all*." She guided the officers back to the foyer. "Have a pleasant evening," Mrs. Larsen told them, and then closed the door quickly.

By now the orange glow of streetlights was creating pockets of warmth in the darkness. A breeze bristled through the branches, and brisk air whisked into the house, leaving Ridley with a chill. Top Hat was now hiding under the couch, closer to the heating vent by the wall. Ridley hoped that her mother didn't spy his fuzzy tail sticking out from underneath the hem of draped fabric there. Mrs. Larsen returned and said,

"Well, now that that's over with!" When no one moved, she cleared her throat, her face turning slightly pink.

Ridley was about to suggest that her mother go back upstairs and continue working on her writing, when Mr. Vernon approached Ms. Parkly. "In all the hubbub, I don't believe I made the pleasure of your acquaintance," he said.

"Oh...the, uh...pleasure is all mine?" Ms. Parkly gave his gloved hand a formal shake. "I'm Helena Parkly," she said, glancing at Ridley and the others with an embarrassed look. "Ridley's new teacher." She gave an awkward wave to the Other Mr. Vernon, who nodded politely.

"So," said Mrs. Larsen. "What now?"

"I'm not sure," answered Mr. Vernon. "Those were quite exciting statements you all made to the police."

Ridley's mother huffed. "Well, Dante, what did you expect? And the police? Again? How many more times will we have to call them before the year is out?"

"Mother!" Ridley chided.

"I'm sorry!" Mrs. Larsen's voice was rising into registers Ridley rarely heard. "It's just that...I don't like *crowds*. And...and I have a book due in only a few weeks....And...my daughter should *not* be gallivanting around...." She brought her hands to her face and shook her head.

Ridley wished she had a room full of stuffed animals to fling at her mother.

Suddenly embarrassed, Mrs. Larsen said, "Excuse me, please." She made her way up the stairs.

When she was safely out of earshot, the Other Mr. Vernon whispered to the group, "Ridley's mother is not wrong."

His husband drew his dark brows together. "I thought I made it clear that you all needed to *not* be seen together?" He didn't sound angry. He didn't sound disappointed. He did, however, sound tired, like Ridley's mom.

"I'm sorry we didn't tell you, Dad," said Leila. "It's just, Ridley had this awful experience today at the inventors' fair in Bell's Landing and we—"

"What kind of awful experience?" Mr. Vernon asked, looking at Ridley.

But Carter continued, "A woman, who was acting hypnotized, smashed up her invention project with a shovel."

"Oh, that *is* awful. I'm so sorry, Ridley."

"But that's not everything," said Leila. "All of us,

over the past few days, have had similar encounters with people who were acting mesmerized. Remember the grocery store?" Mr. Vernon nodded, concerned. "The cashier kept saying, '*What have I done,*' over and over."

Theo spoke up. "And that is what an usher said to me at a concert with my parents, right before he pretended to slip and fall on top of me."

And Izzy added, "Me and Olly too. There was a guest at the resort who ruined our performance in the lobby. He was saying the same thing: '*What have I done? What have I done?*'"

Olly nodded. "I wanted to tell him, '*You ruined our performance! That's what you've done, ya dum-dum!*' But I didn't get a chance."

Mr. Vernon looked at each member of the Magic Misfits as if they had just told him that the magic shop had reappeared and then blown up again. He shook his head at the Other Mr. Vernon. "This is not good. Not good at all."

"It's gone from frightening to outright dangerous, Dante." The Other Mr. Vernon twisted his hands together.

"Ridley thinks that we should start meeting up again

in public," Carter blurted out. Ridley slapped the arm of her chair in frustration, and a puff of smoke erupted from a hidden compartment under her seat. (This was one of Ridley's favorite ways to express her annoyance. Much simpler than something that could be misconstrued, like *words*, don't you agree?)

"Sorry, Ridley. Didn't mean to spill the beans. It's just..." Carter turned to Mr. Vernon. "What if Kalagan never left Mineral Wells?"

"We don't even know what he looks like," said Leila.

"Sure we do!" said Olly. "He wears a top hat and a cloak!"

"She means the man's face," Ridley quipped. "Can you describe him, Mr. V.? All we've ever seen is that old picture of the Emerald Ring club."

Mr. Vernon rubbed at his brow. "I haven't seen Kilroy Kalagan since we were kids. And even back then he was always changing his appearance, his hair color, his style. I don't think I'd recognize the man today if he were standing right in front of me."

Carter stood. "So, what do we do, Dante? Should the Magic Misfits stay hidden? Should we stop meeting *at all*?"

"It seems to me that this is not about the Magic Misfits," the Other Mr. Vernon considered.

"Indubitably," Mr. Vernon replied. "What's going on now is about something larger."

"That is what I said," Theo mentioned. "Kalagan wants to—"

SMASH!

The window at the side of the house crashed inward. Splintered glass scattered across the living room rug, and something landed in the middle of the floor with a house-shaking *WHUMP*.

Leila and Carter yelped and jumped up onto the love seat. Theo pressed himself against the nearest wall. Olly and Izzy clutched each other and covered their heads. Mr. Vernon raised his cape to shield Ridley, while Ms. Parkly watched astonished from the foyer.

"Away from the windows!" said the Other Mr. Vernon.

"Is everyone all right?" asked Mr. Vernon.

The group checked themselves. Thankfully, they had all been out of the way of the flying glass.

A moment later, Ridley wheeled over to the object that had further shattered their evening. Reaching to the floor, she struggled to pick up a heavy parcel wrapped in butcher paper and brown twine. "Careful, Ridley," Mr. Vernon warned, but she had already untied the string and was peeling away the wrapping. Underneath, there appeared something gritty and red. Ridley brushed her finger against it, gathering up pink dust. It was a brick. Ridley rested it in her lap, then turned the butcher paper over. Someone had scrawled out a message in waxy black pencil.

Ridley read it aloud, *"What...Have...I...Done?"* She glanced up at the group, her lip beginning to twitch with fear. She looked to the broken window. A jagged hole glittered like monster teeth in the light of a nearby streetlamp. Outside, a breeze whipped up a few fallen leaves, making them skitter across the sidewalk, sounding like claws.

Mrs. Larsen called out from upstairs. "What in the

world was that noise?" Coming down the stairs, she shrieked at the mess in her living room.

Mr. Vernon put his hand on her shoulder and said, "I'm sorry, my dear woman, but I believe we need to call the police again."

NINE

After the police showed up at the Larsen house for the second time that evening, after they examined the scene of the crime, asked even more questions, and confiscated the brick and the note, after Leila retrieved a frightened Top Hat from under the sofa, after Mr. Vernon promised to get everyone home safely and then led them all out the door, after Mrs. Larsen, Ms. Parkly, and Ridley cleaned up the broken glass and patched the window with a sheet of plastic, Ridley finally headed through the doorway underneath the stairwell and down the ramp to the little room her father had set up for her a few years prior. She flicked the light switch, and a couple of old Edison bulbs glared from their cords hanging over her workbench.

The walls were black, and the room felt like little more than a large closet, but Ridley took pride in the fact that the space belonged only to her. Shelves and cabinets flanked the space. Extendable grabbers were propped against a few tables so that Ridley could access containers and tools in corners and up high. Her father had called this *the lab*, which made Ridley smile. To think of herself as a mad scientist with an actual lab made her feel powerful and strange. She knew she wasn't *mad*, whatever that meant, but she knew that tinkering on projects calmed her down and helped her think.

And if there were ever a time that Ridley needed to feel calm, this was certainly it.

She examined the plans she'd drawn up at the end of the summer and compared them to the device she had been working on ever since—a big black box with a set of wheels attached to its underside. The contraption lay on the floor beside the table in the center of the small space.

Someone knocked on the door.

"Not now, Mother!" Ridley called out. Couldn't she have even a few minutes to work without being interrupted? But the door opened anyway. "Oh. Ms. Parkly…" Although she'd wanted to be alone, she still felt an odd disappointment that it wasn't her mother who'd come to check on her. "I thought you'd left."

"Not yet!" said Ms. Parkly. "Do you mind?" She ended the question by gesturing toward the space, asking if she could enter. Ridley nodded reluctantly. After spending a few moments trying to figure out where to sit down, Ms. Parkly awkwardly perched on Ridley's workbench, slipping on a sheaf of papers before righting herself again. "Silly me!" she said with a giggle.

"What is it?" Ridley said, turning over the pages on which she'd carefully drawn out her plans.

"I wanted to see if you were okay."

"I guess I am." Ridley held up her arms. "No cuts. No scratches. No bruises."

"Ah, well, I didn't really mean that."

Ridley looked into her teacher's eyes, searching for a clue as to what was really going on in her head. "Where's my mother?"

"She's calling some people about coming to fix the

window tomorrow. I offered to stay over, but she said no." Ms. Parkly glanced at the box on the floor. Ridley tried to move forward to block her view. It was meant to be a secret, especially from someone as puzzling as her teacher. "Do you want to talk about what all happened?"

"Not really."

"Do you want to talk about...anything? I find it's helpful when I'm feeling...flustered, frustrated, or downright ferocious!"

What on earth is this woman talking about? Ridley wondered. Her mother? The librarian's attack? Carter's uncle?

Or the *brick*?

"Something that helps me when I'm feeling stuck is looking at a problem from a different angle. If I think that I know the only solution, it can make me feel like I'm out of control when that solution doesn't work. Or when no one else wants to do it *my* way."

"Uh-huh," said Ridley, unsure where she was going with this.

Ms. Parkly's sharp nose seemed to point down at her. She crossed her legs under her long wool skirt and placed her hands on the workbench, leaning back casually. Unfortunately, the workbench was covered with tools and screws and the like, and her teacher jumped up after almost impaling herself on a board with nails sticking out of it. "Eep! I'm good, no blood, I'm fine. Anyway, I was just saying that I think it's good that you have this space to yourself. Finding a way to focus has always helped me sort myself out. You're a clever girl, Ridley. You like to think things through. You'll find a way to solve these puzzles."

"Thanks, Ms. Parkly," Ridley whispered. She didn't want to enjoy the note of confidence, but she had to admit that after everything that had happened that day, it felt nice.

It made her think about how Carter's uncle had spoken to him that afternoon. How he had made apologies and promises. And still, he had chased them through the village. Ridley remembered the lies that Sandra Santos had told the Magic Misfits. How Mick and Emily Meridian had tried to manipulate Theo. How even Dante Vernon seemed to have trouble telling the truth, the whole truth, and nothing but the truth.

Ms. Parkly's eyes roved toward the papers on the bench that contained the plans for Ridley's secret project.

The connection Ridley had allowed herself to feel with her teacher instantly snapped. How could she have been so stupid? She snatched her papers away and held them to her chest. She felt like there was a red poker in the middle of her brain. What came out of her mouth next came so hot and fast she couldn't contain it. "Are you working for Kalagan?"

Ms. Parkly flinched. "Kalagan?" A nervous giggle escaped.

Ridley knew this wasn't part of her plan, but she couldn't help herself. "Kalagan," she repeated. "Are you working for him?"

Ms. Parkly shook her head slightly. Strands of her strawberry-blond hair began to rise with static. "I'm not sure what you're talking about."

"Get out," said Ridley.

"But I—"

"Get out, I said!"

Her teacher

pressed her lips into a line and gave a curt nod. "Sorry to bother you. I'll be back in the morning."

When the teacher was gone, Ridley returned to her project, horrified at herself for letting her guard down—but also for snapping at Ms. Parkly. She picked up her screwdriver and slowly began attaching the contraption's door to the lid as she'd planned. And when she finished, almost all the anger that had been coursing through her had evaporated.

HOW TO...

Turn a Rubber Band into an Eraser

If you happen to have your own laboratory underneath the stairs in your home, I'm sure you'll have no trouble finding an abundance of rubber bands and erasers to use for this next lesson. No? No laboratory? Well, then I'll wait a moment longer for you to ask an adult where they keep these things. Hurry back! We're about to transform a rubber band into an eraser, though it will take a good amount of practice.

WHAT YOU'LL NEED:

  A rubber band

  A small rubber pencil eraser

  A long-sleeved shirt or jacket

TO PREPARE:

Place the rubber band around your right wrist, hidden just underneath the cuff of your sleeve.

Stretch the rubber up across your palm and pinch it between your thumb and index finger.

Hide the eraser by palming it underneath your ring finger on your right hand.

HELPFUL HINT:

Keep the top of your right hand facing the audience so they can't see what's behind it.

STEPS:

1. Use your left hand to stretch out the rubber band, showing it to your audience.

2. Let go of the band with your left hand, but keep enough pressure on it with your thumb and index finger so that it looks like you are holding the rubber band in your right hand.

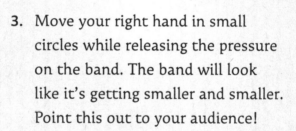

3. Move your right hand in small circles while releasing the pressure on the band. The band will look like it's getting smaller and smaller. Point this out to your audience!

4. Once the band has "shrunk down" almost all the way, let go so the band snaps down to your wrist, hidden inside your cuff.

5. At the same time, slowly turn your right hand over, revealing the eraser. Hold up both the eraser and your open right hand, so that your audience thinks you've turned the rubber band into the eraser!

6. Take a bow!

TEN

That night, Ridley had trouble sleeping. Something inside her was changing, shifting, transforming, and she kept waking with worry, checking that she was still in her own bed, in her own skin.

By the time she opened her eyes in the morning, there was a heaviness in her stomach. After her exercises, bath, and then breakfast, she realized that the heaviness was guilt. As Ms. Parkly rang the doorbell, Ridley didn't know how she would face her teacher after being so horrible to her the previous evening.

But then, Ms. Parkly tripped while coming into the foyer, as usual, smiling at Ridley and rolling her eyes. When they sat in the sunroom and opened the books Ms. Parkly had brought, it was as though Ridley's outburst the previous night had never happened. What was strange, however, was that the weight in Ridley's stomach was only growing heavier.

The lessons that day were about the history of locomotives in the United States and the decimation of the American buffalo. Ms. Parkly had Ridley read essays about the Dust Bowl and then write one about FDR's federal tree-planting program. They finished in the afternoon with a long talk about the practicality of algebra.

Ms. Parkly went on her way after the contractors arrived to replace the broken window in the living room.

It was then that Ridley's belly brick became almost unbearable, because that was also the time she knew she needed to sneak to the supply shed behind the town hall and see if the other Misfits showed up.

Stopping near the front door at a little after three o'clock, Ridley listened for the sound of her mother typing in the office upstairs. *Clack-clackity-clack.*

Yup, writing away as she always is and will be for hours, Ridley thought as she slipped outside and moved quietly along the creaky ramp that twisted down from the front porch to the sidewalk.

The sky was overcast, and the lack of sunshine made Ridley wonder if she'd worn a warm enough jacket. But pushing the wheels of her chair got her blood pumping, and soon her cheeks were flushed. Groups of kids were walking home from their various schools and bus stops, and briefly, Ridley wondered if she might be better off having actual classmates, not being so dependent on the Misfits as her only friends.

She checked around corners of houses and through the windshields of parked cars to make sure no one was watching or following her. A few blocks farther brought her into the village proper. She crossed Main Street and the town green, trying to not look at the spot where Vernon's Magic Shop had once stood, but she couldn't help it. The emptiness of the plot made the weight in her stomach seem to twist, and she winced.

The town hall was straight ahead. She veered around the front steps and made her way down the long drive toward the parking lot. The supply shed sat at the rear of the lot against a tall wooden fence. Unsure if any of her friends were inside, Ridley took a quick breath.

Carter and Leila's public school should have let out twenty minutes prior—Theo's private academy about ten. Olly and Izzy attended classes with a tutor for the resort-employee families up at the Grand Oak. It would take them some time to hike down the hill.

Ridley continued across the wide lot, steering clear of the few cars parked there. She felt exposed until she reached the rear of the rusting tin structure.

A moment later, from the other side of the shed, footsteps scuffed across the parking lot. Ridley tensed, hovering her finger over the switch that would throw her chair into automatic reverse. There was a scratching sound overhead as something scratched against the shed's roof. Looking up, Ridley saw a little pink beak, black eyes, and a white feathered head peer over the edge at her. Then came another. And another. Theo's doves! He must have taken them for a walk... or a flight, rather.

The sound of footsteps stopped at the corner of the shack, and Theo peered around at her. "Oh, thank

goodness," he said. "How are you?" Ridley released a shaky sigh, which was all the answer he needed. "Me too. I could not concentrate all day. My mind kept flipping back to Kalagan. And Carter's uncle. And the brick."

"I keep thinking of the mesmerized people." Ridley shuddered. "And the shovel that woman used to attack my project at the fair."

Now came the sound of rapid footfalls. Someone was running toward them. Soon Carter and Leila dashed around the corner of the shed.

"Hey, hey!" said Leila. "Sorry for the holdup."

"We took the long way," said Carter. "Stuck to the shadows."

A moment later, something flew over the wooden fence and fell to the ground in front of Ridley's chair. A yellow-and-green-plaid duffel bag. Two faces appeared at the top of the fence—Izzy and Olly, full of smiles.

"Howdy!" said Izzy, pulling herself up and swinging her legs over.

Olly followed, landing on the pebbly ground with an *oof*. "I meant to say that," he said, brushing himself off.

"And *I* meant to say howdy," said Izzy.

Ridley realized that the brick in her belly had suddenly eased, that wondering if her friends would still come despite the danger was at least half the reason she was so anxious all day. "What's in the bag?" she asked.

"Our disguises, of course," offered Izzy. She zipped the bag open and revealed a treasure trove of clothes, hats, sparkly accessories, and assorted trappings. "Our old disguises didn't make it out of the rubble at the magic shop, so we dug through our storage space at the resort and found costumes from our grandparents'

old *Golden Family Revue*. Some of the stuff in there was *golden* indeed!"

"Good enough for us to put on a show!" said Olly.

"Oh, we're gonna put on a show, all right," said Ridley, feeling impatient to get started. "But it's not going to be one that will end in applause."

"Then maybe it should start with some!" said Izzy. She began to clap and hoot.

Ridley dashed forward so quickly, she almost ran over Izzy's toe. She tried to cover Izzy's mouth. "We're trying to be discreet!"

"Oh, right," said Izzy. "Sorry!" She covered her mouth herself.

They divided up the costumes, then took turns inside the old shed. When Carter came out, he looked the very picture of *Dandy*. His blond hair was slicked down with black shoe polish, his eyes shaded by giant dark circular sunglasses. He wore a slim black-and-white-striped suit and shiny shoes. Around his neck, he'd draped a brown cashmere scarf, fluffed out to cover his chin.

Leila had pulled her hair up underneath a white

handkerchief. She was draped in a long white apron tied at the waist and stained pink in a few small spots. Under one arm, she'd tucked several parcels, wrapped in brown paper, dripping with a gory-looking juice. "I'm a butcher's assistant!" she claimed with a grin, as if she had finally achieved a life goal. When the others stared at her in shock, she said, "There was some pink paint in the supply shed. I thought we were going for realistic?"

Theo wore overalls and a train engineer's striped cap. "I have been working on the railroad?" he offered rather meekly.

"Aaaaaall the live long daaaaay!" Olly and Izzy chorused as they reappeared looking very much like themselves.

"Where're your costumes?" Ridley asked.

"We're wearing them!" said Olly. "I'm her."

"And I'm him!" Izzy finished.

"Considering that you two already dress exactly alike, maybe you could try again?" Ridley suggested.

Crestfallen, the twins went back into the shed and came out a few minutes later looking like a pair of bird-watchers, wearing vests with several pockets and Indy fedora hats. They both held large binoculars before their faces and pretended to gaze at the sky. "Hey, look!" said Izzy, pointing to the roof of the shed. "Doves!"

When it was Ridley's turn, she pulled an old burlap sack out from a dusty corner of the shed and draped it over the back of her chair to hide all the features that might give her away. From the twins' duffel, she removed a gauzy cloth and wrapped her hair, tying it in the back so that it looked like a turban on her head. She put on a pair of thick rimmed lenses that made her look like she was wearing a pair of magnifying glasses. They hurt her eyes, but she was willing to suffer for the cause. For a dress, she found a piece that reminded her of something Sandra Santos might have worn, all tassels and stars and fringe.

The group gathered at the rear of the shed to check one another out. "We look ridiculous," said Ridley.

"The question is," said Theo, with a grin, "do we look like ourselves?"

ELEVEN

"We'll leave the parking lot separately," said Ridley. "Take different routes. Remember, it can't appear as though we know each other."

"I won't even look at you," said Izzy.

"*I* won't even look where I'm going!" said Olly.

"Well, don't step into traffic!" said Ridley. "Just be careful, everyone. Let's meet in the lobby of the library. Ten minutes?" She glanced at her watch.

"Ten minutes," said the others. They left the lot one by one, not looking anything like they had when they'd entered. Ridley kept a lookout for anyone who might be spying on them, waiting until the whole group blended into the pedestrians on Main Street.

Mineral Wells Public Library—a wide single-story brick building with a steeply pitched slate roof—was only a few blocks from the town hall. Overgrown evergreen shrubs grew up before many of the library's tall, thin windows.

(Never underestimate seemingly irrelevant areas of foliage, my friends. An overgrown evergreen shrub makes an excellent hiding place, if you don't mind a few pokes here and there!)

Ten minutes after Ridley had started her countdown, the entire crew had gathered in the library's lobby. "Did anyone see you?" she asked.

"I am positive *many* people saw us," said Theo. "But I do not believe they were paying attention."

"Excellent," said Leila. "Okay, now how do we want to handle this?"

"I'll track down the librarian at her office," said Ridley. "You guys stay out of sight but be ready to help."

"I will stand just outside the office doorway," said Theo. "None of us should do this completely alone."

Ridley nodded, then headed past the checkout desk

and into the stacks. Theo walked beside her while the others separated into different aisles. The two made quite a pair—he in a conductor's uniform, she wrapped in fabulous fabric—but Ridley wasn't thinking about that. Her heart pounded as she imagined confronting the woman who had destroyed her project. What if the librarian had held on to that strange shovel and was keeping it under her desk in case Ridley showed up? What if she was *still* mesmerized?

Ridley approached the door. A name was marked in gold leaf on the rippled glass: *Iris Maloney—Librarian*. As she knocked, Ridley glanced at Theo, who nodded encouragement. She felt safer knowing the others were behind her, hidden by the shelves.

"Yes?" came a voice from inside the office. "Who is it?"

Ridley cringed and pushed open the door. At her desk, the librarian glanced up from a ledger. When she saw Ridley in the doorway, she gasped.

"Ridley," the librarian whispered, as if she were seeing a ghost. Clearly her disguise wasn't working. "What are you doing here?"

"Mrs. Maloney. Hello." Nervous, Ridley lifted the

thick lenses and propped them on her head. "I came to ask you some questions."

Mrs. Maloney stood. "Of course, sweetheart. Come in. I'm so sorry about what happened....Can you forgive me?"

"I think I need to understand what happened a little better before we can get there." A worried look flashed behind the woman's cat-eye frames. "Why were you at the college yesterday?"

Mrs. Maloney answered immediately. "I was visiting my granddaughter. Lauren's a freshman, studying fine arts. She thought it would be fun for us to check out the projects at the inventors' fair." Mrs. Maloney's eyes darted up and to the right—a sign, Ridley had read, that someone was lying. Before Ridley could confront her, the librarian went on, "I'd had a headache that morning, and by the time we made it to the fair I was feeling dizzy. I don't even remember approaching you. I especially don't remember...doing what I did."

Ridley decided to play Mrs. Maloney's game. "You looked pretty out of it," she said. Mrs. Maloney's pink cheeks turned red. "Do you remember what you were saying just before you attacked me?"

"The police told me it was something like, '*What am I doing?*'" The librarian's eyes darted up again like those of a liar.

She was starting to make Ridley's skin itch with anger. "*What have I done*," said Ridley. "Those were the exact words."

"Oh. Yes. Right."

"Did someone tell you to say that to me? Did someone tell you to pick up that shovel and ruin my project?"

Mrs. Maloney shook her head. "I—I don't think so." Eyes up and to the right. "I had a headache."

Ridley set her jaw. "Have you ever been hypnotized?"

"Pardon me?"

"Mesmerized. Hypnotized. Are you susceptible to suggestion?"

Eyes up. "I don't understand."

Ridley had had it. "Kilroy Kalagan told you to attack me. *Didn't he?*"

"Who? What?" Mrs. Maloney's voice dried into a squeak.

"Kalagan. A man dressed in a dark cloak and a top hat. Did he approach you at the fair?"

"No, I would have remembered—"

"What about a woman in an argyle sweater-vest and a long wool skirt?" Mrs. Maloney shook her head. "You don't know Helena Parkly?"

"Maybe…Doesn't she live here in town? I remember signing up someone with that name for a new library card sometime within the past few months." After a moment, she added, "Isn't she your teacher?"

Ridley groaned. This was going nowhere! She wanted to tear off her head-wrap and throw it at the librarian, then scream that she was a liar and a bully. But then she thought of Theo standing just outside the doorway. She thought of Ms. Parkly's advice from the previous night, about looking at problems in another way. Finally, she thought of her mother, screaming at the cheesemonger yesterday about screwing up her order.

Ridley cleared her throat and eased her chair a few inches forward. "Mrs. Maloney," she said. "You probably know about the troubles that I and my friends have faced over the summer. You were in the park on the night that Mr. Vernon's shop…You saw everything. You know how much it hurt us." Ridley looked into the woman's eyes. "Can't you please…just tell me the truth?"

Mrs. Maloney's voice came out like a piano stripped of its strings. "I can't," she whispered.

"You can't tell me what you know?" Ridley asked. "Or you can't tell me *the truth*?"

"I can't..." Mrs. Maloney held a trembling hand to her throat. "I'm sorry, Miss Larsen. Would you excuse me? I'm not...feeling well."

Ridley had to bite back asking if she felt another "headache" coming on. "If you find that you're suddenly feeling better, would you please give me a call?" Ridley grabbed a pencil from the desk and jotted her phone number down on Mrs. Maloney's blotter.

Red faced and wobbly, the librarian nodded a goodbye.

★ ★ ★

In the lobby, Ridley asked her friends, "Could you hear us?"

Everyone said yes.

"Very suspicious," said Carter.

"Not very helpful," said Leila.

"She was *also* not very funny," said Olly, throwing his hands up in mock exasperation. "She's gotta work on her timing."

"Not everyone can be a comedic genius," Izzy told her brother. "Not even you." Olly made a face and then pretended to faint.

"She was lying," said Ridley, ignoring him. She told the group about how Mrs. Maloney's darting eyes were a sign. "I thought about going at her harder." She glanced at Theo. "But then...well...I didn't think it would help. Maybe she'll come around."

"Very wise," Theo agreed.

"On to the next attacker," said Carter.

"The grocery store isn't far from here," said Leila. "We could talk to the cashier who dumped our food on the ground."

"Done and done," said Ridley, ready for answers.

★ ★ ★

A few minutes later, after taking different routes through the village, the group met at Wentworth Market on Pine Avenue. This time Ridley hid along with Theo, Olly, and Izzy while Carter and Leila approached a young man at the register. Ridley positioned her chair around the corner from where the bread was stacked on some wire shelves.

"Bradley?" Leila said.

"Can I help you?" answered the young man at the register. He wore a dress shirt and necktie, with a dark green apron. His black wayfarer glasses made him look like he read lots of thick books about nerdy subjects.

(Not that that's a bad thing. Nerdy subjects are some of the best kinds!)

"Do you recognize us?" Carter asked. Bradley squinted, then shook his head. Carter pulled down the scarf. "How about now?"

"What do you want?" Bradley sounded annoyed. His expression said he knew exactly who they were.

"We've got some questions about the other day," said Leila. "When you dumped all of our groceries on the floor?"

Bradley smirked, then checked himself. "Yeah. Sorry about that."

"Did someone put you up to it?" asked Carter.

Offended, Bradley replied, "Of course not."

"Then why?" Leila wondered aloud. "Why would you do that?"

"I don't remember."

"It only happened last week," said Carter.

Bradley straightened his tie. "Calling me a liar?"

This was not going well, thought Ridley. *Would she have to rush over there and put Bradley in his place?*

"Have you ever been hypnotized?" Leila went on.

"I really need to get back to work."

"Did *Kalagan* put you up to it?" Carter tried, his voice rising slightly.

The cashier's eyes bugged out. His thin lips turned white.

"Please," Leila begged. "We're in trouble. And it's not only *our* family. If Kalagan continues to wreak havoc on Mineral Wells, yours might end up suffering too."

Taken aback, Bradley blurted out, hushed and rapid, "Stop asking questions."

Carter and Leila stared at him, unsure. "What was that?" Carter asked.

"It's not *safe*," Bradley added before quickly changing his disposition. He put on a cheery smile as easily as Carter had put on those enormous sunglasses. "Thank you and come again!" he finished.

"*What's* not safe?" Leila whispered.

"Thank you and come again!" Bradley repeated, louder. It almost sounded like a threat.

Once outside, Ridley waved for the group to follow her behind the garbage bins and out of sight.

"That was creepy," said Carter.

"He said *it's not safe*," said Leila. "What did he mean?"

"Just what he said," Ridley answered. "He's got a secret that he's scared to share."

"Now *I'm* scared," Izzy whispered, shivering.

"Are you sure you're not just cold?" Olly asked.

As Izzy considered that, Ridley went on, "It doesn't sound like the answer of someone who's been mesmerized. He *knows* something. Maybe even what Kalagan actually looks like." She glanced toward the store's entrance. "I wish there was some way we could get the cashier to talk."

"*And* the librarian," said Carter.

"If not them," said Theo, "we still have a couple others who might."

"Is the arts center open right now?" asked Leila.

"No," said Theo. "But I can call them later this evening to ask about the usher."

"So we head up to the resort," said Ridley.

"We question Quinn, the concierge," said Leila. "See if she knows the name of the guest who heckled us and his room number."

"See you all at the Grand Oak lobby?" Ridley said.

"Be sure to blend in when you get there," Izzy suggested.

"But don't blend *too* much," Olly quipped. "Otherwise, people might think you're making milkshakes." His eyes went wide. "Mm. *Milkshakes*...Leila, do you think your poppa will blend us some—"

"Clock's ticking!" Ridley reminded him before scooting out from behind the garbage bins.

They split up. Carter, Theo, and Leila went off on their own. Ridley, Olly, and Izzy took the resort's trolley.

Once situated in the carriage, Ridley glanced out at the passing storefronts, keeping her face partially hidden by her hand. Olly and Izzy sat in the rear, pretending to not know each other. Thankfully, they were the only ones riding. As the trolley puttered up Main Street, Ridley heard the twins gasp.

Olly whispered, "Is that...?"

Izzy answered, "I think so!"

Ridley saw who they were talking about. The greasy ponytail gave it away. Carter's uncle Sly was peering through the window of the empty shop where Meridian's Music used to be.

"Shh," said Ridley. "Don't make a scene." But to Ridley's horror, the trolley's driver suddenly rang the bell, and Uncle Sly turned toward them. Before she could cover her face or look away, he noticed her and smiled.

His lips were cracked, and his teeth had a grayish tinge. As the trolley turned the corner, he lifted his hand in a small salute.

TWELVE

At the hotel, Dean, the bellhop, held the door open for Ridley and the twins.

Dean had been working at the Grand Oak for as long as Ridley could remember. His eyes were darkened with tired circles, and his hair was almost entirely gray, but he always managed to greet the guests politely and had even assisted the Misfits with their plots and plans over the past few months. "Afternoon, Miss Larsen," he said, tipping his hat to her. He even tried to straighten his stooped spine in acknowledgment. He smiled at the twins. "Olly. Izzy."

"You're not supposed to recognize us, Dean!" said Izzy, entering the resort's lobby.

"Why not?" he asked, confused.

"We're in disguise," said Olly. Ridley turned her wheels so fast that her footrests smacked into Olly's calves. He yelped and then realized what he'd said. "I mean...*costume!*"

"You should know by now that we *LOVE* costumes, Dean," said Izzy, pulling her brother away from the bellhop.

Ridley untied the wrap from her head. If Dean recognized her, so would everyone else up here. The best she could do to protect the Misfits at this point would be to move far from the twins and pretend she wanted nothing to do with them.

"What brings you to the Grand Oak today?" Dean asked her.

"Research," Ridley answered without hesitation. "I'm doing a project with my new teacher about the local economy. And since the Grand Oak is one of the biggest employers in the area, I thought I'd start here. Have you seen the manager? I was hoping to interview him."

"Oh, Mr. Arnold is always running around," said Dean. "But I'll keep an eye out and let you know."

"Thanks!" Ridley answered, trying to sound non-chalant.

Passing by the sofa where the twins were sitting, she noticed them talking to a man and a woman who were both dressed in Grand Oak uniforms. She'd never seen them before. Ridley overheard the man ask, "Why are you two festooned like a couple'a bird-watchers?"

Ridley navigated toward the large fireplace at the far wall. She slipped the burlap cloth off the back of her chair and folded it onto her lap. Then she removed her fake glasses and shoved them under the burlap. She tried to capture Izzy's attention to signal that they should give up the game, but Izzy was too focused.

Minutes later, Carter came through the door wearing his dapper disguise followed by Leila in her pink-splattered apron. Ridley made sure to catch each of their gazes before casually moving around the corner of the fireplace and out of sight of the employees and guests. A few minutes later when the others found her in the shadows behind a potted fern, she whispered, "Thank goodness, you made it."

"Why wouldn't we have?" Leila asked.

"Carter's uncle was snooping around the old Meridian's Music shop. We worried that you might run into him."

"Sly was at the music shop?" Theo asked with a worried look. "What was he doing? Trying to break in?"

"He was just peeking in the window," said Izzy.

"Maybe he wanted to buy a harmonica," Olly offered. When the others just stared at him, he blushed. "Or a tuba! I don't know what he plays."

"We're safe," said Carter.

Leila whistled with relief. "Thank goodness!"

"Too bad our disguises were pointless," said Ridley.

"What do you mean?" Theo asked.

"Uncle Sly recognized us right away! And Dean. Honestly, I think we're drawing more attention this way. We've got to come up with a new way to transform ourselves."

"I've always wanted to try prosthetics!" Carter crowed.

"Carter!" Izzy whispered. "How can you think about food at a time like this?"

Carter snickered. "I mean, like fake noses or scars made from makeup. Dante used to sell some basic kits in the magic shop."

"I haven't worn my fake nose in years," said Ridley. "Maybe it's time for a new one."

"I'll have my dad order one for you," said Leila. "He's been trying to set up a new version of the magic shop. A fake nose is as good a place to start as any."

Leila uncovered her brown hair, untied the white apron from around her waist, and placed the wrapped fake-meat parcels behind the fern's pot.

Carter couldn't wipe the shoe polish from his hair, but he took off the sunglasses and tucked them into his pocket and unwound the scarf from his neck.

The twins removed their vests and turned them inside out. To Ridley's surprise, they were reversible and were now a matching green-and-purple plaid. She wasn't sure if that was better or worse than what they'd been wearing before. Either way, the change made them look like themselves again, which hopefully would stop other hotel employees from asking why they were playing dress-up.

"I noticed Quinn isn't at the concierge desk," said Carter.

"Gregor and Tara mentioned that they hadn't seen her in a couple hours," Izzy replied.

"Who are Gregor and Tara?" Ridley asked, thinking

of the couple who had been speaking with the twins a few minutes prior.

"Gregor is my mom's dance class assistant," said Olly. He did a little tap flourish.

"Tara is my singing instructor," said Izzy, trilling the end of the sentence.

"Perfect," said Carter, with an annoyed harrumph. "With Quinn gone, how are we going to get information about the guest who bothered you?"

Ridley peered back into the lobby from behind the thin leaves of the fern. Her eyes landed on the old bellhop, who was standing hunched near the front doors. "I can think of someone else we all know who might be willing to help."

The other Misfits stayed back as Ridley made her way across the lobby again. She could feel their eyes on the back of her chair. "Hey, Dean," she said. "I've got a question for you."

"Haven't seen Mr. Arnold yet," he answered, shaking his head.

"Not about that." Ridley cleared her throat. "Were you around the other day when a guest here in the lobby was making a scene?"

Dean's face went pale. "I most certainly was."

"Would you happen to know what room that guest is staying in?"

"Oh, he's long gone. Checked out later that afternoon. Didn't even stay the night."

Ridley nodded jovially. "Good thing! I'm sure Mr. Arnold doesn't want people like that hanging around here."

"None of us do."

"Hey, you wouldn't happen to know the guest's name, would you?"

Dean shook his head. "I remember bell-hopping his bags out of room 412." Then he looked at her funny, as if something had just occurred to him. "Does this have to do with that research project you mentioned?"

"Uh...*yes*. Yes, it does."

Dean raised an eyebrow. "And I suppose you want me to find out about him for ya?"

"In the name of research?" Ridley grinned.

Dean glanced around the lobby. He gave a non-committal grunt before shuffling off toward the desk where Quinn usually sat. "Wait here," he said over his shoulder. A couple of minutes later, after digging around in a drawer behind the concierge station, he returned with a scrap of paper on which he'd scrawled some words. He handed it over.

"Fred Tithe," she read aloud.

"His middle name was in there too, but I didn't know if you needed it. I thought it was pretty weird."

"It won't hurt," Ridley answered, flicking her hand near the arm of her chair, a pen appearing between her fingers and thumb.

Dean leaned close and whispered, "Punier."

"Punier?" Ridley echoed. "What kind of name is Punier?"

"My thought exactly," said Dean. He broke out into laughter, his voice crackling like static. "Puny. Punier. *Puniest!*" He guffawed.

"Thanks for this," she said, backing away. "I'll—uh...I'll let you know how the rest of my project goes."

Dean composed himself. He waved her closer. "I know it's not for a research project."

"Of course it is!" said Ridley, putting on a surprised voice.

"It's nice to see you all together again," he whispered.

Ridley's face flushed. "I don't know what you mean."

"Your magic friends," he said conspiratorially. "You're all dressed up today. You're rehearsing for another show! It's what the twins were hinting at earlier, wasn't it?"

Ridley felt cornered. What if Dean talked to someone? "It's a secret," she said quietly. "No one can know. Not yet. We've got some preparing to do."

Dean pretended to lock his lips. "Your secret's safe with me," he said, then tipped his hat and went back to his place near the door.

THIRTEEN

Have we really reached thirteen already? Ugh! An unlucky number for an unlucky chapter!

Since the Magic Misfits need all the luck they can get, let's fill these pages with as many lucky things as we can think of.

I'll start:

1. Pennies
2. Rainbows
3. The laughter of babies
4. Four-leaf clovers
5. The ringing of bells

6. Birthday wishes
7. Spare eyelashes lying in someone's palm
8. Black cats (Yes, I know many might consider them *un*lucky. But this is utter poppycock. They are, in fact, supremely lucky.)
9. Blue birds
10. A pinch of salt over your shoulder
11. The number 11
12. Drummers drumming
13. Mr. Vernon's ace of spades card

Oh no! I can only think of thirteen things! Even *more* unlucky!

Quick, come up with one more lucky thing, and then let's turn away from this stressful section.

14. _____

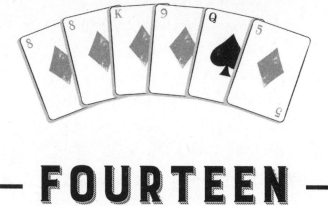

FOURTEEN

"*Fred Punier Tithe*," Leila read off the paper when Ridley handed it to her.

The group had moved into the secluded lounge that was filled with the potted plants, just off the lobby and outside the kitchen where Leila's poppa worked.

"Fred P. Tithe doesn't sound like a real name," Carter added.

"My thought exactly," said Ridley.

"*Tithe*," Theo echoed. "That's an actual word. Do any of you know what it means?"

"A tithe is a kind of tax," said Ridley. "A payment.

But that...doesn't make sense. Does it?"

Leila offered, "Maybe Mr. Tithe's *name* is supposed to be a message from Kalagan. We know he's a crook, a con artist. Is he expecting a payment from us? Payment to make him and his mesmerized goons leave us alone?"

"Why wouldn't he just come out and *tell* us?" said Carter. "If he wants a payment, it would be helpful to know what kind he wants!"

"He likes to play games," said Leila. "To make us decipher his puzzles. To make us wonder if we actually know what we think we know."

Theo squinted at Ridley. "You look like an idea is blooming somewhere in there."

"Ooh!" said Izzy. "I love when Ridley's ideas bloom. They're so pretty."

"We're looking at the wrong part of the name," Ridley responded. "Dean said it himself. What kind of name is *Punier*?"

"I don't know," said Olly, eyes wide with expectation. "What kind?" He looked like he was expecting Ridley to answer with a punch line.

Leila gasped. "An anagram."

"Anna-*who*?" Olly asked, disappointed.

Izzy patted his shoulder. "They're saying that the rude guest gave the hotel a made-up name."

"Not *only* that," said Theo. "But a made-up name whose letters can be rearranged to spell something else."

"Like a secret message," said Olly. "*Anagram!* I remember that from when the ventriloquist visited and there was that secret message in his marquee poster. *Magic Misfits Crumble*?"

"Ex-*actly*," said Ridley.

Izzy shook her head. "But I like my eggs over easy."

Olly looked excited to keep this going. "I like *my* eggs—"

Ridley held up her pen like a sword. "The sooner we start decoding, the sooner we can figure out who this guest actually was."

They broke into groups of two, Ridley providing everyone with pencils and scraps of paper.

Ridley and Theo worked together. They managed to scramble Fred's name to say: *PETRIFIED HUNTER.* And *THE PURIFIED RENT.* And *FEED THEIR TURNIP.*

Ridley was about to suggest to the group that they go and ask the Other Mr. Vernon if he kept turnips in a special place in his kitchen—a place they might search for another clue—when Carter and Leila let out a couple of small squeals. "What is it?" she asked them. "What did you find?"

Carter held out his and Leila's list of anagrams. At the bottom, Ridley read: *UNDER THE FIRE PIT.*

Olly and Izzy *oohed* and *ahhed.*

"That *has* to mean something," said Theo. "Is there a *fire pit* here at the Grand Oak?"

"Behind the outbuildings," said Leila. "There's a clearing in the woods and a circle of logs for sitting and in the center—"

"The ash pit," Ridley finished. "Where the staff builds a campfire every night during summertime."

"We'll need a shovel," said Carter.

A thought flashed through Ridley's mind—a memory of the librarian raising the shovel of the future and bringing it down onto her project.

"There should be one out near the groundskeeper's shed," Leila answered. "But first, shouldn't we go get Dad and Poppa? Tell them what we learned?"

Ridley shook her head. "We're breaking their rules by meeting here. What if they send us all home?"

"But we have been breaking the rules since the end of the summer," said Theo.

"That was breaking the rules in the correct way," said Carter. "Now we're breaking them wrong. Ridley's right. The Vernons might get mad."

"Who cares if they get mad if they're the ones who can keep us safe?" Leila said, her usually cheery eyes growing dark.

"But they *haven't* been keeping us safe," said Ridley. "It's why we're in this situation."

"That's not fair," said Leila.

"I don't care," Ridley answered, her voice beginning to rise. Theo cleared his throat, and Ridley took a deep breath. "I'm sorry, Leila. I *do* care. But we've already come this far. We're onto something. Once we figure out exactly what it is, we'll tell the Vernons. Until then...I say, let's go do some digging."

★ ★ ★

Outside, the Misfits followed the paved pathway between the buildings where resort guests spent many an hour participating in summer activities. Now that the days were shorter and the nights cooler, the guests stuck to hiking trails, and these outer buildings were closed up tight—padlocks hung from hasps on the doors, and wooden shutters barred the windows.

In the evening darkness, Ridley felt as though they were walking through a ghost town. Shadows crept out from around the corners of the buildings. Carter carried the shovel they'd taken from the groundskeeper's cache. Ridley wished she'd taken one too. For protection.

The clearing appeared ahead—a grass-covered knoll with a wide circle of cut pine laid out around a small ring of stacked bricks. The fire pit. The *maybe* spot that Fred P. Tithe had *maybe* marked with a *maybe* X. Ridley turned on her chair's light and pointed it toward the bricks. She listened to the woods that surrounded them for the sound of a snapped twig, a rustle of dry leaves, a sudden hush—anything that might indicate danger. Any number of undesirable people could be out there. One of the mesmerized people. Or Carter's uncle. Or Kalagan himself. But all she heard was a high wind moving harshly through tall branches and the whisper of pine needles brushing endlessly against one another.

Carter peered into the brick ring. "Ashes and dirt." He began to clean it out. Minutes later, the bottom of the pit was clear. He waved everyone forward. They worked together to lift the brick floor out from inside it, revealing raw ground below.

Theo held up one of the bricks to Ridley's light. "Does this look familiar?"

Smash! Ridley heard the sound of splintered glass, and the previous night came whooshing back to her. "You think whoever broke our window used one of these?" she asked.

"It stands to reason," Theo answered. "Aren't we playing with fire?"

"No, Theo," Izzy said gravely. "We are playing with *bricks.*"

"I tried to juggle bricks once," Olly added. "I don't recommend it."

Ridley turned to Olly. "Why would you ever…juggle a…" She sighed. "Forget it. Look, I really don't want to be out here any longer than we need to be. Carter?" She nodded to the shovel perched against the ring of bricks. "Want to see what's down there?"

"Do I?" Carter asked with a gulp. He picked up the shovel and then pitched the tip into the earth under the fire pit. He closed his eyes, striking at the dirt again and again, tossing it out onto the grass. Ridley directed the light so that he could see what he was doing.

When he'd dug down at least two feet, Izzy cried out, "What's that?"

In the hole, something glistened from underneath a scattering of dirt and pebbles and a couple of writhing night crawlers.

Theo reached into the hole, brushed away the dirt and pebbles, and pulled out a chestnut-colored oilcloth sack. Whatever was inside was heavy enough to pull at the bottom and make it swing pendulously in his grip.

The Misfits all stared, none of them willing to break the spell.

Ridley couldn't stand it. "Would you just open the sack already?" she practically shouted at Theo.

"Whoa," said Izzy, taken aback.

"Are you all right, Ridley?" asked Olly.

Ridley held her breath. If even the *twins* were struck by her ferocity, she needed to dial it down a notch or three. Theo glared at her, then he tossed her the sack. She caught it before it could land in her lap. She glared back at Theo. "What if there's something dangerous inside?"

"Go ahead and *open the sack already*," Theo answered, his voice deliberate. Ridley felt her face burn.

"We can open it together," said Leila, trying to

smooth over the rough patch Ridley had stumbled into.

"Thanks, Leila," she answered, ignoring the warmth in her cheeks. Together, the girls pulled at the leather drawstring that cinched the top of the sack. Carter, Theo, Olly, and Izzy perched on the edge of the brick ring like an eager audience. Leila lowered the sack toward the arm of Ridley's chair so that the light was directed into the opening, then she reached in and pulled out two small, rectangular wooden boxes.

As soon as Ridley saw them, she felt a shock of recognition. Two memories sprang up from the past summer—the morning that Bosso's goons had stolen items from each of her friends, and then the afternoon when the Misfits discovered Sandra Santos's secret stash under the rock in the basement of the Grand Oak's neglected West Lodge. One of the boxes had belonged to Carter's father. The other had been Sandra's. What were they doing buried back here?

"Puzzle boxes," said Olly, leaning forward to examine them.

"Just like ours," said Izzy. Ridley flinched, confused.

"Wait a second," said Leila. "You two have a box too?"

"We found one here at the hotel a few months ago," said Olly. "We tried to get it open, but we couldn't figure out how."

"Weird," said Carter. "I still have my dad's. His initials are inlaid into the wood on the side. Never got his open either."

"And I held on to Sandra's," said Leila. "The one from the Emerald Ring's lair in the basement of the West Lodge. It's still locked up tight."

Ridley was startled. "I thought…You mean *these* aren't *those*?"

Carter and Leila shook their heads. "Look," said Carter, taking both boxes from Leila. "My dad's initials were LWL. Sandra's are AIS." He showed the new boxes to the group. "There are different inlaid letters on these."

Theo scratched at his forehead, looking guilty. "I have one too."

Ridley nearly fell over backward. "You do? How?"

"At the end of the summer, I got a letter from Emily Meridian. She sent me a key to her father's store. I found a package in Mick's workshop, wrapped up and

marked with the message *Keep Safe*. The initials on my box read: MXM. Mick Xavier Meridian."

Leila held up one hand and ticked one finger down for each name, for each box. "LWL. *Lyle Wilder Locke.* Right, Carter?" Carter nodded. "AIS. *Alessandra I. Santos.* MXM. *Mick Xavier Meridian.*" She glanced at the twins. "What about you two? Were there initials on the box you found?"

Izzy sat up straight, as if she were being quizzed. "Ours was BOB."

Leila ticked down another finger. "Bobby O. Boscowitz. Also known as B. B. Bosso."

"I thought maybe it just belonged to someone named Bob," said Olly.

"Every one of these boxes belonged to the members of the Emerald Ring," said Ridley. "Mr. Vernon's old magic club." She held out her hands to Carter, and he placed the ones from the oilcloth sack on her lap. "Each member must have had one with their own initials." She turned the new boxes over, looking for the inlay she knew would be there. "Look! This one is marked VDV—"

"Virgil Dante Vernon," Leila whispered. "My *dad*."

"Your dad's first name is *Virgil*?" Olly and Izzy said together.

Ridley examined the other box. "KAK." She felt a shiver shoot from the top of her head to her shoulders and then down her arms. "Kilroy A. Kalagan." The lamp on Ridley's chair flickered. "Is there anything else down there?" she asked, nodding at the hole in the fire pit.

Carter checked. "Doesn't look like it."

"Good. Then let's get out of here. This place is creeping me out."

The group made their way back to the main lodge, stopping near the groundskeeper's shed to return the shovel Carter had borrowed. The porch light from the Grand Oak's side entry filtered past them, making Ridley feel safe. Or safer than she'd felt out by the clearing.

"What does all of this mean?" asked Theo, the oilcloth clenched in one fist. "The name that Dean gave us led to these new puzzle boxes. The rude guest. His anagram name. Was it a clue sent to us by Kalagan? Or maybe someone else?"

Ridley ran her fingers over the engravings on the boxes in her lap. Lines swooped and swirled in haphazard shapes. "Would you all mind bringing your puzzles boxes out here? I want to examine them."

"Mine is back home," said Theo.

"That's fine," said Ridley. "We can get that one later."

Carter, Leila, Olly, and Izzy went up to their rooms as Theo and Ridley waited silently in the lounge, tucked behind the large leaves of several elephant ear plants. Minutes later, the other Misfits returned, puzzle boxes in hand.

"They're like the heads of the Darling Daniel dolls," said Ridley, tapping on them. Hollow. "Maybe I should break them open."

"And what if there is something delicate inside?" Theo asked. "Or something dangerous. Chemicals? Powder that could make us sick?"

"I'll put on protective gear," said Ridley. "I've got plenty back at my lab."

"I'm with Theo," Leila said. "There's got to be another way."

"Yeah," Carter agreed. "They're *puzzle* boxes after all. Besides, I don't want anyone to smash something that belonged to my father."

Ridley felt her temper flare but doused it quickly. She had a recent experience with people smashing her possessions, so she understood how Carter must feel. After a moment, she said, "Okay. I'm with Theo too."

"You *are*?" asked Izzy.

"*Are* you?" Olly echoed, although in a slightly different order.

"Really?" Theo asked, looking truly shocked.

"Really," Ridley went on. "You asked, 'What does all of this mean?' And that's what we need to find out. Our next best option is to go back and talk to Dean. Maybe he can get a little bit more out of Fred P. Tithe's records. A payment method. An address. A phone number. Even if *Tithe* is a made-up name, *some-one* had to do the making up. Right?"

The others agreed.

Smiling, Ridley added, "And afterward, I can take the boxes home and see if I can solve their puzzle."

To her surprise, they agreed with that too.

When Ridley scanned the lobby, Dean was nowhere to be found. Quinn had returned to the concierge desk, so Ridley approached her instead. Quinn's freckles made her appear kind, which was a good thing, since her job was about helping befuddled guests order taxis and get directions and make dinner reservations and book tickets for all sorts of events down in the village. Her blond hair was pulled back in a ponytail, which poked out from underneath her hotel uniform's cap. "Ridley Larsen!" she said. "It's been a long time!"

"Hi, Quinn. How're things?"

"Peachy keen and served with cream."

Ridley glanced around the lobby again. "Say, you didn't see where Dean went off to, did you?"

Quinn frowned. "I did not. Is there something I can help you with this evening?"

"Maybe," Ridley answered, thinking quickly how to navigate everything she needed to keep secret.

"Earlier, Dean was able to track down the name of a guest who'd been staying in room 412. Fred Tithe. I had a question for Mr. Tithe regarding this project I'm working on, and I was wondering if you might be able to tell me how I can contact him? Or maybe *you* could contact him for me. I know it's a lot to ask...but it's important."

Quinn looked puzzled for a moment, then said, "Hold on a sec." She hurried off to the front desk. Ridley followed. Quinn picked around in what looked like a box of receipts. Then she pulled a large notebook out from under the desk and pawed through it. After a few seconds, she shook her head. "You said the name was Tithe?" Quinn asked. Ridley nodded, her skin going cold. "Sorry, Ridley, but it doesn't appear that a Mr. Tithe stayed in room 412."

"Oh, well, maybe I got the room wrong."

"No, honey, you misunderstand me. Nobody with that name has *ever* stayed here at the Grand Oak Resort."

FIFTEEN

Ridley flinched, forcing herself to not peer over her shoulder at the spot where her friends were hiding. "But this is the name Dean gave me. Fred Punier Tithe."

"I don't know what to tell you." Quinn made a sad smile. "Maybe he was messing around. We're not really supposed to give out guest information to just anyone. Not that you're *just anyone*, Ridley, but...you know what I mean."

"I guess I do," Ridley replied, trying to not look as confused, or as embarrassed, as she felt. As she made her way back toward the fireplace, those emotions started to transform, and by the time she reached her friends, she'd become full-on furious. "We've been had," she spat out.

"By whom?" asked Theo.

"I'm not sure," Ridley answered. "By Dean? By Quinn? By someone else?" She quickly explained what Quinn had told her, and watched her friends' faces turn grimmer.

Leila began to fidget. "I say that's enough for today. It's late, and Dad and Poppa are probably wondering where we are. Even though they've been busy trying to rebuild the magic shop's business from up here at the resort, they've also been pretty protective lately."

After agreeing to come down to Ridley's tomorrow afternoon to look closer at the puzzle boxes, they all said their goodbyes.

Ridley called her mom to come pick her and Theo up. "You didn't even tell me you'd *left*, Ridley," Mrs. Larsen had snapped. "I'm in the middle of the penultimate chapter and now I have to step away *again*.... Where are my keys? I could have sworn— Oh, there they are....Have you had lunch yet? I don't have much at home...and if you'd given me some sense of what you'd be doing today, I could have planned...."

Eventually Mrs. Larsen hung up the phone and arrived in her mint-green Plymouth a few minutes later, looking exhausted. There were dark marks under her eyes, and her hair was frizzed out. Ridley figured she'd worked through the day without glancing in a mirror. "What's all this?" Mrs. Larsen asked when Ridley handed her the oilcloth sack filled with the five puzzle boxes to put in the trunk.

"Research?" Ridley answered.

To her relief, Mrs. Larsen shrugged.

In the back seat of the car, Ridley whispered to Theo, "Can you bring out Mick's puzzle box when we get to your house?"

"How about tomorrow instead? My mom and dad are probably going to be upset that I stayed out after dark."

Ridley pressed down on her annoyance—and then realized that she was only annoyed at being annoyed. "Understandable. I'll work on what I can tonight, and then we'll see if Mick's box helps anything when you bring it over."

Theo smiled. "Nice," he said. As they sat in silence, Ridley wondered if he'd been commenting on her plan for the puzzle boxes, or if he'd been commenting on *her*. Either way, it certainly felt *nice* to be getting along with her best friend again.

Once inside her house, Ridley made straight for the small doorway beneath the foyer staircase. "There's some fruit in the kitchen," her mother said before starting upstairs toward her office. "I've got to get back to the book."

"It's fine," Ridley called out. "Not hungry just yet anyway."

(Ah, I do wish Ridley would have a piece of fruit. Apples, pears, bananas—they are so very *good* for you. Let's all take a quick break and find something to snack on, shall we? I'm craving a piece of dragonfruit myself.)

In the lab, Ridley arranged the puzzle boxes on the table in the center of the room. There was something to the strange markings that gleamed from the inlaid wood—something Ridley knew she was missing and that might help her discover what was inside them.

She glanced at the box of tools on a shelf, considering a small handsaw. She remembered the promise she'd made to her friends at the hotel—that she wouldn't break them open. But it wouldn't take much just to see...

No. The Misfits were the most important thing right now. She wouldn't let them down. And who knew? Maybe the point of the boxes had nothing to do with what was *inside* them. Maybe they had a different purpose entirely. She couldn't be sure, however, until Theo brought the final box over tomorrow afternoon.

She glanced instead at the secret project she'd been working on since the end of the summer—the long crate that was lying on the floor beside the workbench. Reaching for her tools, she attached another wheel to its underside and realized that she'd been constructing a *different* kind of puzzle box all this time.

She had a feeling that, very soon, it might just come in handy.

✦ ✦ ✦

The next day stretched out like a rubber band.

Ridley could barely concentrate on the lessons that Ms. Parkly had planned for her. In the back of her mind, she wondered if maybe her teacher could have been responsible for the Misfits finding the puzzle boxes. Ridley made sure to not mention their discovery to her.

When the doorbell rang shortly after three o'clock, Ridley was still in the middle of some reading that Ms. Parkly had assigned, so her teacher answered the door. "Come in, Theo," Ridley heard her say. The bell rang twice more—once for Leila and Carter, and the other for Olly and Izzy. Ridley directed them to the back of the house.

Mrs. Larsen called down from the top of the stairs. "Who keeps ringing the doorbell?" In the kitchen, the Misfits hushed. Ridley felt a flash of fear that her mother would find her friends gathered together, flip out, and then send everyone home. Ms. Parkly must have seen Ridley's worry because she ran to the foyer to intercept Mrs. Larsen before she could come down past the landing. *Was she actually trying to help them?* Ridley wondered.

"Sorry about that," said Ms. Parkly, giggling characteristically. "Ridley and I were just finishing up for the day. A lesson about...er...sound!"

"Right!" Ridley called out from the living room, her chest tight. She glanced through the kitchen door and waved her friends toward herself, silently directing them to stand against the wall, away from her mother's view.

"Oh, Mrs. Larsen!" Ms. Parkly proclaimed suddenly. "There was something I wanted to ask you about. In *private*. Could you join me outside?"

Ridley wanted to cheer at the sight of her mother following her teacher through the front door. Was Ms. Parkly familiar with the concept of misdirection?

"Quick!" Ridley whispered. "Follow me." Within seconds, the Misfits had assembled inside Ridley's lab, safe and sequestered. "Sorry about the sneaking around," Ridley told her friends. "My mother is liable to lose it if she finds a bunch of people in the house."

"Nice of your teacher to distract her," Carter said. "Did she do that to help us?"

"Yes, but I still don't trust her," Ridley replied. "We can't trust anybody these days."

The Misfits nodded grimly as they gathered around the table in the center of the room where Ridley had arranged the five puzzle boxes.

Theo handed over the final one. "Just like I promised."

"Thank you. Late last night, I was playing around with the boxes when I had a realization." She reached out and flipped each box onto its side. "When they're placed in the right order like this, the decorative inlay lines up to form a picture."

Leila held her hand to her mouth. "Is that...?"

"Jeepers," whispered Carter.

"It looks like a ring," said Theo.

"With a jewel," said Izzy.

"An emerald," Ridley added with a smile. "See the green pieces of wood?"

"Shiny!" Olly exclaimed.

Ridley was so excited, she could barely hold it in. "Exactly. But the puzzle was still missing one piece." She held up the box that Theo had brought with him, the one with the MXM marking. "Ready?"

"You bet," said Carter.

"I'm worried," said Leila.

"Should we cover our heads?" asked Izzy.

"I cover my head when I cough," Olly added.

Ridley reached out and placed the final box in the center of the stack. The inlaid decorations finally matched up to form a whole image—an emerald ring spread out across the six old boxes. Immediately, strange sliding sounds came from inside them. This was followed by six separate clicks.

"What happened?" asked Theo.

"Nothing," said Carter, crossing his arms. "Maybe all of this was misdirection." He glanced around nervously. "Wait...what *aren't* we paying attention to?"

"Look," said Ridley. Keeping the other boxes in place, she reached out to the one closest to her. She pulled the top of the box lengthwise, and a compartment opened, the lid sliding within finely crafted wooden grooves. The others gasped. "The boxes needed to be together in order for the inner workings to be released. Could be some sort of system of magnets?" She went up the stack, sliding each of them open, and then pulled them all apart. "Go on," she told them. "Take one."

Theo, Leila, Carter, Olly, and Izzy each grabbed a piece of the emerald ring design from the box lids.

"What's inside?" asked Leila.

"Only one way to find out," said Carter.

Ridley felt slightly nervous, as if she were sticking her hand into the mouth of a wild animal. To her supreme disappointment, she felt nothing inside the box. "It's empty?"

"It is not," Theo answered. Pinched between his forefinger and his thumb was a scrap of yellowing paper. The paper looked ancient. Weathered. There appeared to be writing on it in faded black ink. "This was stuck to one side of the box. Check again."

The others followed his directions, and a moment later, each of them was clasping a similar scrap. "What are they?" Leila asked, holding the paper closer to the light. Her jaw went slack. "This says, '*Sincerely, Dante Vernon.*'"

"It's a letter," said Ridley.

"From my dad," said Leila.

"Torn into six pieces," said Carter.

"Addressed to whom?" asked Theo.

"Let's put them back together," said Izzy. "Just like a jigsaw puzzle."

Olly scowled. "Izzy, this is no time for games!"

"It's not a game, silly," Izzy answered. Then she reconsidered, "Well, it *is*. But it's also *not*. Never mind! Hurry!"

The Misfits each placed their scrap onto the table, matching up the lines of ink just like Ridley had matched the inlay on the boxes. Moments later, the letter was whole again.

Leila leaned forward and began to read the message aloud. *"Dear Kilroy—"* She gasped. "It's a letter to Kalagan!"

> *Dear Kilroy,*
>
> *I am sorry beyond words. I feel like a fool even attempting to explain what happened.*
>
> *For a long time, I have been jealous of your skill. That is why, when we all had the opportunity to shine at the Mineral Wells talent show, I just had to win that finale spot. I decided to make the Ring believe that your act was too dangerous by ensuring that your fire trick would burn brighter than it was supposed to. But the blaze got out of control! It wasn't supposed to be like that. You must believe me.*
>
> *I consider you a brother, Kilroy. Brothers fight. They quibble. But they always forgive. None of this was my intention. I feel that my heart has been changed. If I could switch places with you, my friend, I would. In a flash.*
>
> *Sincerely,*
>
> *Dante Vernon*

Leila stared at the page in her hand. "I don't understand," she said. "My dad would never have written this. He would never have *done* this. Starting the fire at the Grand Oak that killed those people?"

"It's got to be fake," said Carter.

"But his handwriting—"

"That is one of the easiest things to fake," said Theo.

Olly and Izzy glanced at each other with worry.

Ridley took a deep breath. "Let's forget about the content of the message for now."

"How?" asked Leila, her voice quivering.

"By considering where it came from. The complicated steps that someone took to make sure it reached us. This is obviously Kalagan's doing. And it's obviously another ploy to hurt us. To hurt Mr. Vernon. To drive us all apart."

"But what if it's true?" asked Carter. "What if Mr. Vernon is the real villain?"

Leila's eyes brimmed over. "Carter!" she cried out.

"We'll deal with that when it matters," Ridley said, reaching for Leila's hand. "Right now, we need to figure out the trick. Six puzzle boxes. All of them open only when they are placed side by side. Whoever had this letter, whoever tore it into six pieces, once must have had *all* the boxes. That's the only way those paper scraps could have ended up inside them."

"It must have been a really long time ago," said Theo.

"I've had my father's box with me since I was a toddler," said Carter, nodding.

"Tell me again how we came by the rest of these?" Ridley asked.

"I found Sandra's in the basement of the West Lodge," said Leila.

"Me and Izzy found Bosso's up at the resort," said Olly.

"Yeah, but only after someone led us to it," Izzy added. "Remember that scavenger hunt?"

"Not really," Olly answered with a shrug.

"Mick Meridian's box was in his empty music shop," said Theo.

"Right," said Ridley. "And didn't Emily send you a key so that you might find it there?"

Theo nodded slowly, sudden suspicion etched onto his brow. "Could Kalagan have forged that letter? Made sure I got the key to the shop?"

"Yes," said both twins. "He could have."

"Then that leaves the final two," said Ridley. "Mr. Vernon's and Kilroy Kalagan's. Which, as we know, came to us yesterday evening. Doesn't it seem like someone timed it so that we would receive this letter *right now*?"

"However it got to us," Leila said, "shouldn't we bring it to my dad?"

"Do you really want to confront him?" Ridley asked. "What if he tells you something you don't want to hear?"

"That he did start the fire? He could just as easily tell us the letter's a fake!"

"How would we know if he's telling the truth?" Ridley asked.

"My dad is not a liar!"

Ridley took a deep breath. "I'm not saying he is. I don't want to believe any of this either." The thought of their beloved mentor doing something so horrible made her feel sick to her stomach. And she knew that if she upset Leila further, the Misfits might scatter. Maybe that's exactly what Kalagan had been hoping for. "I'm saying…we need to be careful. Maybe it would be better to learn a little more about Kalagan's intentions before we all walk right into what might be a trap."

"Should we at least try to talk to Dean?" Theo asked. "He was the one who gave us the name that led us to the fire pit."

"As good a place to start as any," Ridley answered.

"Do you know if he's working at the resort today?" Carter asked the twins.

"Gah!" said Olly. "If only one of us was psychic!"

Izzy shrugged. "We can call up there and find out."

"Or...yeah, we could do that," Olly finished with a nod.

SIXTEEN

Ridley phoned the resort and learned that Dean was off for the evening. After they tracked down his phone number, they called him at home, but there was no answer. And after they checked the phone book for his address, the Misfits snuck out of the Larsen house and made their way into the village toward his house. On the way, Leila continually burst into tears. Carter kept saying that everything would work out in the end. But Ridley wasn't so sure. She felt like Kalagan's influence was starting to infiltrate her own mind, sending her down bramble patch tunnels to dead end cliffs.

The best she could do was scan the street, making sure that no one was following. So far, she'd noticed three cars parked at three separate corners with suspicious-looking people just sitting behind the wheels and staring straight forward.

On Emory Street, they came to a small, white, Cape Cod–style cottage with black shutters, and a number on the mailbox that matched the one listed in the phone book for Dean. Unlike the other houses on the block, there was no landscaping in front, and the lawn was untidy and overgrown. Ridley had a strange feeling about the place.

"Do we knock?" asked Theo.

"He didn't answer when we called," said Carter.

"Maybe he was in the bathroom," Olly suggested. "My dad can stay in there for hours, it seems."

Ridley rolled her eyes. "Ring the doorbell at least."

Theo climbed the step and pressed the button. A buzzer sounded from somewhere deep inside. They waited and listened, but after several seconds, there was still no response.

"Leila, do you have your lock picks?" Ridley asked.

Leila raised an eyebrow. "Really? Right here? In front of the whole town?"

"Maybe there's a door around back?"

At the rear of the house, Leila paused, tools in hand. "This feels wrong," she said. "It's Dean's house. He's our friend."

"I don't think any of us is arguing that breaking into a house is the best option," said Ridley. "But if the house was on fire, would the firefighters stand here and wonder if they were doing the right thing by smashing open the door?"

"Dean's house is not on fire, Ridley," said Theo.

"Even so," Ridley went on. "This is an emergency. And who knows? Maybe Dean's in there and needs our help."

Leila released a shaky breath. Within seconds, she had the back door open. The Misfits crept inside.

"Hello?" Ridley called out. "Dean?" It felt slightly less like an invasion if he knew they were coming. They entered into a dimly lit kitchen with peeling linoleum on the floors and a dank smell that made Ridley wrinkle her nose. She opened the cabinet underneath the sink to find it mostly empty. Same with several drawers that contained only a single set of silverware and a few cracked plates. Ridley's strange sense about the house only grew stronger.

The front room contained a ratty-looking green velvet couch and a couple of folding tray tables, as well as a large console radio and a tall bookcase against the wall. Through a doorway, there was a twin bed with blue sheets tucked in military style and a blanket folded neatly at the foot. There were no frames hanging on the walls, no artwork or mirrors or photographs— nothing that gave away any part of Dean's life, which, come to think of it, Ridley realized that she really knew nothing about.

"Come on," said Carter. "Let's go. This is pointless."

Ridley was about to turn back toward the kitchen when something behind the bookcase caught her eye. A line of wooden molding was attached to the wall. She pointed it out, and Olly and Izzy moved the case carefully out of the way, revealing a door.

"Whoa," Ridley whispered. "There must be something inside that he doesn't want anyone to see."

Leila tried the knob only to find it was locked, but she made quick work of it, and then pushed the door open. Darkness stared back at them. Ridley switched on her chair's light, which shone into what looked like a cramped room. Or maybe a large closet. Its floor was covered in machinery and what looked like rolls and rolls of tape. A small table held radio parts.

Carter gasped. "Is that what I think it is?"

"I already told you I'm not psychic," said Olly. "What do *you* think it is?"

Carter stepped aside and allowed the rest of the Misfits to get a better look.

"I'm confused," said Izzy. "What kind of gadgetry are we looking at?"

"It is a radio receiver and a recording device," said Theo. "The kind of receiver someone would use if they had distributed radio transmitters throughout an entire town, hidden inside the wooden heads of ventriloquist dummy dolls."

Leila groaned. "We knew that someone at the hotel had set all of that up. Could it have really been Dean?"

"Looks like it," Ridley said, her brain buzzing.

"Can someone explain to me what's going on?" Carter asked. "This is getting super complicated."

(I agree. Don't you? *Super* complicated! Then again, some of the best magic tricks are the same way—complex. To perform these types of tricks, you must be prepared. You must also know what came before so you can take the next step. Thankfully, Theo will now remind us all!)

Theo began, "Everyone remembers when Mr. Whispers arrived at the hotel at the end of the summer, right?" The Misfits all nodded. "Of course. And we *also* remember the dolls that started appearing around town, the ones that someone at the resort had decided to use to promote Mr. Whispers's ventriloquism show." Another nod from the group. "The dolls looked like the ventriloquist's dummy, Darling Daniel."

"And when I managed to crack open their heads," Ridley added, "I found that someone had placed radio transmitters in all of them."

"After we confronted Wendel Whispers, we found out that he knew nothing about it. He was so disturbed, he packed his bags and left town."

"But *someone* had been trying to listen in on the conversations of the people of Mineral Wells," Ridley went on. She nodded at the contraption in the closet. "In order to listen, that person would have needed a radio receiver. Just like *this* one." She reached through the doorway and opened a filing cabinet drawer. It was filled with reels of tape. She grabbed one. A name had been written on the side in black marker. *Sheila Fields.* "I know her," Ridley said. "She's friends with my parents."

Ridley picked up another reel and another. Each was marked with a name. Some were of particular interest to the Misfits—there was Iris Maloney, the librarian, and Bradley Nickel, the cashier. Most of the names, however, they did not recognize.

"Is this starting to make sense?" Theo asked. Carter nodded reluctantly. "We'd asked the resort manager, Mr. Arnold, whose idea it had been to hand out the dolls, but he said it had been organized by a committee of employees."

"Which could've included Dean," said Leila, shaking her head with disappointment.

"But the tapes?" Carter added. "Why record a bunch of random people?"

"Sandra Santos said that Kalagan is good at making people do what he wants," said Ridley. "What if his power isn't mesmerism? What if his power is *manipulation*? If he has recordings of people from all over, he wouldn't need to hypnotize them into doing his bidding. He would only need to scare them by threatening to release all of their secrets."

"Elementary, my dear Watson," Izzy said appreciatively.

"Watson?" Olly asked. "Wouldn't Ridley be Watdaughter?"

"That is so messed up," Carter added.

"Then, the people who attacked us..." Leila paused, thinking. "Kalagan must have told them to do it or else he would share his recordings of them."

"They must have done or said some really vile stuff!" said Izzy.

"Not necessarily," said Theo. "Perhaps their secrets are merely things they are not ready to share yet."

"Should we listen to one of the tapes?" Olly asked. "See how bad it is?"

"Of course not!" Leila squeaked. "It would be an invasion of privacy."

"Something that Kalagan has *no problem* with," Theo added.

"Same with Dean," said Ridley.

"I still can't believe it," said Izzy. "He's our friend."

"Should we destroy the tapes?" Carter asked.

"I don't think we can risk having Dean know that we were here. We need to talk to him. Pronto," Ridley said firmly.

"But what would keep Dean from just running away from us?" Leila asked. "He might go tell Kalagan that we're on to him. And he could send all the people he's manipulating after us!"

Ridley paused, then said, "I've been working on a device that would keep Dean from running off. In fact, I think it just might be ready for us to test out."

"You mean like a rope trick?" asked Leila.

Ridley shook her head.

"Something that could make him disappear?" asked Carter.

"Nope."

"I doubt it has anything to do with levitation," said Theo.

"You want to make him laugh so hard, he can't move?" asked Olly.

"What I've been working on is more like a giant version of one of our puzzle boxes," Ridley answered. "I'm hoping Dean will simply step inside."

The sound of a car passing outside made the Misfits jump. "Let's get out of here," Carter said grimly. The friends hurried back to the kitchen, making sure not to bump any furniture or leave a sign that they'd been inside Dean's home. They filed silently out the door, and Leila quickly reset the lock before bounding after the others toward the safety of home.

SEVENTEEN

It took a few days for the Misfits to bring the pieces of Ridley's box up to the ice cave in the woods—which was not far from the resort's fire pit, where they'd found the two final puzzle boxes. They then spent hours reassembling it. Just as Ridley had planned, the box's wheels fit directly onto the train tracks near the cave's entrance. It helped that she'd created much of the contraption on top of an old bootlegger's cart.

Over the course of those days, every time the Golden twins saw Dean in the lobby of the Grand Oak Resort, they brought up the idea of a Magic Misfits reunion show, just loudly enough for him to hear. On Friday night, the twins came right out and asked Dean if he wouldn't mind coming to the ice cave the next morning to help them figure out their most complicated tricks. Being a big fan of the Misfits, Dean happily agreed.

Ridley woke up on Saturday morning with a lump in her throat. She'd said nothing to her mother of what she and her friends were planning that day, and it felt wrong. What if they encountered serious trouble in the ice cave? Didn't Mrs. Larsen deserve to know the danger Ridley was about to put herself in? Didn't the Vernons and the Stein-Meyers and the Goldens? Parents were supposed to keep their kids safe. But what did it mean when kids felt the responsibility to save their families instead?

After her mother helped Ridley with her morning stretches and exercises, they had breakfast and then Ridley announced that she was heading out to practice some new tricks with Theo. Not *exactly* a lie.

"Be careful," said Mrs. Larsen. "The police tell me they still haven't tracked down the hooligan who broke our window...and you know I don't need anything more to worry about these days....Ugh, just *look*

at the hem of these pants...dragging on the ground....
Where's my sewing kit? Wait, Ridley, you must have
homework, don't you? Do I need to have a word with
Ms. Parkly about challenging you more? Where is she
anyway?"

"It's her day off, Mom. And I'll be okay," Ridley
answered. "Me and Theo can take care of ourselves."

Mrs. Larsen paused before heading upstairs to
her office, then offered, "I know you can. You always
have."

Surprised, Ridley didn't respond until her mother
was out of earshot. "Love you," Ridley called softly,
closing the front door behind her.

✦ ✦ ✦

As the Misfits gathered at the mouth of the cave, cold
air belched out from its depths. The chill went right
through Ridley's wool coat.

Long ago, the hotel staff had built a gravel path
that descended to the bootlegger tracks. Ridley struggled over the rough ground, but she had her reasons
for wanting to set up down there. "Hurry," she said.
"Dean could arrive at any moment."

The Golden twins had brought bunting, strings

with triangular flags, and other decorations from the resort's storage rooms. The others set up the performance space. "It's important that he believes we're *actually* preparing for a reunion show," Leila had said the day prior. When they finished, the mouth of the cave looked like the set of a star-spangled, plaid, striped, and polka-dotted resort revue. Ridley looked up at it in awe. Her magic box sat like a set-piece in the center of a theater stage, the shadows and jagged edges of rocks pointing at it as if someone had designed them that way. She half circled the box, checking all of its various compartments, hinges, switches, and wheels, as the rest of the group organized the props they'd brought for the "magic show rehearsal."

Crunching footfalls sounded on the gravel trail. Dean appeared, and Ridley felt her stomach cramp.

(Mine is in knots as well. How about you? This is where things start to get dicey....)

"Hey, all! Wow! This looks amazing!"

"Hi, Dean!" Leila called back nervously. "We're so glad you're here."

"My pleasure," Dean replied. "Where do you want me?"

Leila pointed toward a small boulder at the foot

of the path. "Right there should work for now." She glanced at the group. "Is everybody ready?" The others gave a quick nod and then assembled before the magic box as they'd planned.

Ridley moved into a shaft of sunshine that resembled a spotlight in an auditorium. She tried to transform her worry into excitement. "Surprise! Surprise! The Magic Misfits have returned!" She waited for Dean to applaud. "And what a show we've devised for you! Prepare for thrills! Get ready for chills! Brace yourself for a journey into the mists of magic!"

The crew gave a brief choreographed bow, then broke apart and stood in different parts of the cave, as they had practiced in the days prior. Ridley kept her eyes on Dean the whole time. Was he acting suspicious? Was he suspicious of them? This had to look like a real performance in order for them to get Dean to do what they needed him to do.

Leila went first. She performed the netted-rope trick that she'd done the previous weekend for Ridley's surprise celebration, to wild applause from the one audience member.

Next came Carter. He stepped forward and, with a hand flourish, fanned out a display of what looked like three decks of cards. "I have a secret," he said, keeping his voice low. Still, it echoed around the space. "I have long hidden that I have a twin brother!" The others gasped in mock surprise. Carter grinned and then nodded at the empty space beside him, holding out his hand as if to introduce someone who wasn't there. "And here he is! Go on, Carl. Give the audience a wave."

After a moment, Carter went on, "You may have noticed that my brother is invisible. But he doesn't let that stop him. You ready, Carl?" Carter looked to the empty space again and grinned. "Olly, Izzy, if you would." The Goldens brought over their pink silk cloth and held it up where Carter had indicated Carl was standing.

Carter moved a few feet away but continued to address his "brother" behind the silk cloth. "Like all brothers, Carl and I like to compete. And sometimes we quarrel. Like this morning, when I bet Carl that he couldn't catch all one hundred fifty-six of these playing cards if I tossed them at him. Well, Carl, now's your chance to prove me wrong!"

Carter whipped out the three decks of cards again. Palming them in both hands, he bent the cards and then raised his arms toward the Goldens' cloth. He let the cards fly! They shot swiftly behind the cloth. When all the cards were gone, he continued. "All right, Carl! Let's see how you did!" He nodded at Olly and Izzy, who dropped the cloth and moved aside.

To Dean's shock, the space into which Carter had shot the decks was empty—not a single card was on the ground.

"Oh," Carter grumbled, looking sheepish. "I guess you *did* catch all of them. Sorry, Carl. I was wrong. You win." He held up a hand to his ear. "What's that? Now you want *me* to try to catch the cards? Well, I suppose that's only fair."

Seconds later, from behind the twins' cloth, dozens of playing cards flew at Carter. They shot out so fast, Carter had to cover his head. Soon, the flurry of playing cards petered out and Carter looked over at his "twin" in mock anger. "I wasn't ready!" he shouted.

A pause. Then he added, "Fine, then. You'll help me pick up all the cards when we're done!" The Goldens dropped the cloth again to reveal the empty space behind it, then moved out of the way. Carter grinned, then pretended to grab his invisible brother's hand, which he raised over his head before giving a great bow.

Dean let out a loud whistle. Ridley suddenly felt bad

about what they were about to do to him. But then she remembered everything he had already done to hurt them.

Theo's performance came next. "I too must request the assistance of our beloved friends, Olly and Izzy, and their grandparents' incredibly magical silk scarf. Or is it a caftan? It is so large, I am not sure exactly what it is supposed to be."

"A tent!" Izzy said.

"Bigger than a tent! An elevent!" Olly countered.

"What's an elevent?" Leila asked.

"Nothin'. What's an elevent with you?"

"Whatever the case," said Theo, getting them back on track, "would you mind holding it up one last time?"

Theo went ahead with the trick he'd done for Ridley's surprise. He played his violin and levitated behind the Goldens' magical silk cloth. When Theo's final note resounded into the cave system behind him, coming back out as a haunting sotto voce echo, Dean was so impressed—or was pretending to be—he nearly fell backward off his boulder.

Now it was Ridley's turn. She moved toward her magic box that was standing upright a little farther back, the bottom perched on the remnants of the old tracks. "Thank you, Theo," she said. "For my trick, I shall need a volunteer from the audience."

Dean let out a *huh-yuck* and then looked around, as if maybe some of the other hotel staff had joined him. When he realized he was alone, he pressed his hand to his chest and called out, "Me?"

"If you don't mind," Ridley said, forcing what felt like the largest smile she'd ever worn. She released a latch on the side of her black magic box and the front of it creaked open like the lid of a coffin. Ridley's heart skipped as Dean crossed the entry of the cave.

"In there?" he asked, looking skeptically at the contraption. "What are you going to do?"

"Oh, nothing much," Ridley joked. "Just turn you into a grizzly bear!"

Dean raised his eyebrows. He shrugged, stepped up into the box, and then turned around.

"Comfy?" Ridley asked. Dean chuckled, then nod-ded. Ridley grabbed the edge of the lid and swung it shut. She flipped a switch. Several bolts slid into place, locking the lid tightly.

Ridley finally let her smile drop away.

Dean wasn't going anywhere now.

Not until she let him.

EIGHTEEN

Theo and Leila rushed to Ridley's side of the box; Carter, Olly, and Izzy gathered at the other.

"Can he get out?" Leila asked.

Ridley shook her head. "The bolts are strong. I tested them in my lab."

Carter reached out toward the box, but then drew his hands quickly away. "What do we do?"

Ridley reached up toward the little door she'd attached to the box's lid earlier that week. "We get some answers," she said. Flipping a small clasp, she pulled on a nearly hidden peg and the little door swung open.

Dean's face was framed just inside. He wore a goofy grin. "Hey, all," he said. His eyes flicked to Ridley. "I've gotta tell you I'm not so sure about your trick, Ridley. I don't feel anything like a grizzly bear." He let out another laugh. But when he noticed the anxious expressions that were plastered on the faces of the Magic Misfits, his own grew concerned. "What's wrong? Did I mess things up? Let me out. I'll be better next time."

"I can't do that, Dean."

"Very funny." The lid shuddered as he pushed at it from inside. "Come on, girl. I don't like this one bit. Let old Dean out of here."

"We'll let you out," said Ridley, "if you answer some questions first."

"Ohh," Dean said with a sigh. "This is all part of your act."

Time to get serious, Ridley thought. "No," she said. "It's not."

Through the porthole, the group watched Dean's face pale. "Let me out of here!" he cried. "Help! *Help!*" There were pounding sounds as the old man realized the situation he was in.

"Ridley," Leila said with a whimper. "I don't like this."

"None of us do," said Ridley, trying to hold on to the assuredness she'd felt while building this contraption. "But he's left us no choice."

"I've been trapped in small spaces myself," Leila went on. "Isn't there another way?"

"Help me!" Dean called out again, his voice echoing out of the cave.

"Dean!" Ridley said with all the force she could muster. "You'll be fine in no time. Just answer our questions. Okay?"

Dean trembled. All of the fight seemed to have left him. ""What...what is it you want to know?"

Ridley turned to her friends. "What is it we want to know?"

The Misfits dug in. They piled on the questions faster than Dean could answer them. They asked about the name he'd given them a few nights prior: *Fred P. Tithe*. They asked about the anagram and the fire pit. They wanted to know what Dean knew about the Emerald Ring's puzzle boxes and the letter they'd found inside them. They told him about the radio receiver they'd located in his house and the tapes labeled with the names of the townspeople. They told him they knew he had placed the transmitters inside the Darling Daniel dolls. They wanted to know *why*?

Why had Dean done what he had done?

"Tell us about Kalagan," said Carter.

"Where is he?" asked Leila.

"What does he look like?" Theo wondered.

Ridley continued the grilling. "How can we stop him?"

Dean blinked. He nodded. His expression was one of defeat. "Can I start by saying that I'm sorry?" the old man asked.

"You can start however you like," Ridley replied. "But how we finish here depends on what you say in between." This sounded to Ridley like some dialogue her mother would have written in one of her stories. She kind of liked it.

Dean's eyes welled with tears. "I didn't mean to hurt anyone. I'm a victim too. Just like the Vernons. Just like you kids." Ridley wanted to tell him to *save it*, but she couldn't risk interrupting him. "At the beginning of the summer, someone started slipping notecards under the front door of my house. The cards were mysterious and kinda threatening. They were always signed with the letter *K*. They said stuff like, *I know.* Or *I'm watching.* Or *What have you done?*" Dean swallowed down some saliva. "Those notes...they started getting inside my head. I thought of bringing them to the police, but then I wondered if maybe the police had something to do with it, so I held off. I wondered if the person leaving me the notes wanted money from me, which I thought was pretty silly, considering the state of my piggy bank.

"One night, shortly after that diamond heist here at the Grand Oak, I boarded the trolley for home. I didn't notice the person who was sitting behind me until I felt a prick at the back of my neck and a hushed voice at my ear, warning me not to turn around. I was terrified, but I obeyed. He told me his name was Kalagan. He slipped an envelope onto the seat next to me and told me to open it. Inside were some letters that I'd written in my youth—letters that I've regretted writing ever since. I'd rather not say what they were about, but I knew then that I would have to do whatever this mysterious man on the trolley asked me to do. And I did *all of it.*" Dean let out a little sob.

"With equipment that he provided, I set up the

radio receiver in my old closet. I set up the recording device. Under Mr. Kalagan's instruction, I managed to convince the hotel manager to book that ventriloquist, to reach out to Mick Meridian to create those dolls to Mr. Kalagan's specifications, to put the transmitters inside their heads, and then make sure they got into the hands of as many townsfolk as possible. You saw what happened. You figured it out. Mr. Kalagan told me what words to add to the ventriloquist's marquee poster before it went to the printer. That anagram that threatened you kids. *Magic Misfits Crumble*? Trust me, I didn't want to do it. After what happened to the magic shop, I thought about leaving town. About starting over somewhere else. Changing my name. Changing everything about me. But...it takes money to do that. I was trapped.

"He knew you'd all come asking around about that guest who messed with Olly and Izzy last week. When you did, he had me give you that mixed-up name. He had me bury those boxes out in the fire pit, knowing you'd figure out his puzzle and then—"

"You keep saying *he had you do this*, *he had you do that*." Ridley felt it was safe to finally try and get a word in. "Did you ever see his face?"

Dean shook his head. "He was always in the shadows. His hat brim tilted downward, his high collar hiding the rest of him."

"What does he want?" Carter asked. "Why go through the trouble of blackmailing almost everyone in town, just so he can get to us? A bunch of kids!"

"You made him angry!" Dean answered. "Kept ruining his plans! You were also a means to an end. To getting to Dante Vernon. That's why Mr. Kalagan had me record all those conversations around town. Without the members of his Ring to help him—you kids keep getting in the way—he needed a new kind of army. Mr. Kalagan says that Dante Vernon is the *true villain*. That Dante wears a mask of kindness that hides jealousy and anger and selfishness!"

"My dad is nothing like that!" Leila yelled.

Dean blinked. "I...I don't know what to believe. Mr. Kalagan says we know nothing about your father. Based on what he told me was in Vernon's letter, I might have to agree."

The Misfits were quiet for a moment. Not even Ridley could argue with that part.

Dean's voice grew even quieter. "What he wants is to get Vernon's followers, the members of his Magic

Circle, to see the truth. And that includes you kids. You might think he hates you, but you've got it wrong. He only wants to *help* you get out from Vernon's lies."

The tone of Dean's voice had changed. The sound of it prickled Ridley's skin. It was like he was becoming someone whose eyes might glaze over as he came at her, fists raised, chanting, *What have I done? What have I done? What have I done?*

Theo must have noticed it as well. "How do you know so much about what Kalagan believes? About what he wants and all that?" Dean shook his head, looking confused. "I mean, if you are a victim, *like us*, why do you sound like you are on his side?"

"He...he told me all that stuff. It sounded like it was true!" Dean stammered. He glanced desperately at Ridley. "Now will you let me out? I don't feel so good. I promise: I'm on your side now. Mr. Vernon's side. The *right* side."

Something was telling Ridley to leave Dean where he was, to have Carter and Leila go up to the resort and bring the Vernons down here. She didn't trust him. But she didn't know which part of his story to not trust the most.

But before she could respond, there was a

crunching sound at the mouth of the cave, closer
to where the gravel path ended and their makeshift
amphitheater began. Ridley glanced over to find the
silhouettes of three people. On the left stood a tall,
broad man with a big head and even bigger arms. His
khaki pants were pulled high, held up by thin leather
suspenders. Ridley remembered seeing him around
town, maybe hanging out in one of the parks with
his family. On the right was a shorter woman whose
broad shoulders made her look like a brick wall. She
wore denim overalls and a white button-down shirt
with the sleeves rolled up, her arms bulging with

muscles. Another anonymous face from the mix of people living down in the village.

By their fixed expressions, Ridley knew the man and woman were members of Kalagan's mesmerized mafia. The biggest clue that this was the case, however, was the figure who stood between them. Although his face was still hidden in shadow, she knew exactly who he was.

The black top hat and the high-collared cloak gave him away.

NINETEEN

"Kalagan!" Leila shrieked.

"Stay away," Olly yelled. "We know karate!"

"We do?" Izzy asked a little too loudly. Her brother shot her a desperate look and she added, "Oh! Yes, we *do*...know...that...." Then she put up her hands as if ready to give anyone who came close enough a really good chop.

Carter widened his stance and made another two decks of cards appear in his palms, ready to bombard one of the attackers with their sharp edges and slippery surfaces.

Theo readied his bow as if it were a sword. Or a wand.

Leila clapped her hands over her head and when she brought them apart, she was holding a length of white rope.

And Ridley squared herself to the trespassers, her own hands hovering over a number of buttons and switches on the arms of her chair.

The Magic Misfits were ready to fight!

The man in the top hat stepped away from the goons who were flanking him and held his hands out, directing them to keep back. There was something dismissive about the smooth way he moved that made Ridley's esophagus burn with rage. His voice echoed forth, low and gritty and somehow suddenly familiar. "Take it easy."

Where had Ridley heard it before? She remembered the night of the talent show and the explosion, when Kalagan had appeared, mocking and mimicking all of them in the parking lot behind the darkened church, using a voice that sounded like Mr. Vernon's, but shifted and changed at his whim.

"Say, Ridley, why don't you let the old man go?"

the voice came again, now wearing an almost amused lilt. "He's *ancient*. Locking him in there all this time? Seems cruel. No?"

Ridley dared to glance back to the opening in the lid of her magic box. Dean mouthed, *Please*. Guilt heated her body, and she was surprised that Kalagan's suggestion had gotten to her so quickly and thoroughly. Maybe he *did* have a mesmerist's power. She edged her chair backward, flicked the switch on the magic box that released the bolts, then swerved quickly out of the way.

When the lid swung open, Dean practically fell to the ground. He caught himself on his hands and knees, then with a great groan, managed to stand as far up as his old bent spine would allow. He heaved a sigh. "I'm so sorry."

Ridley didn't know if he was talking to *them* or to *Kalagan*.

The Misfits parted as Dean eased toward the mouth of the cave, glancing back every few steps, as if he weren't sure he should leave the kids alone. Or maybe to see if Kalagan minded him leaving. But Kalagan's focus was only on the Misfits now. Ridley's throat burned as Dean disappeared over the top edge of the cave's mouth.

"Let's chat, shall we?" Kalagan said. "I hear you have questions."

"Leave us alone, you creep," Carter spat out.

"There is no need for names, Carter. I thought you were better than that."

Ridley watched as a blush turned Carter's face red. She could tell that Kalagan's words had struck a nerve with him as well.

"We've got nothing to say to you," said Leila, doubling up the white rope on her fists.

"Oh, but I think you do. You must! I know you've finally received my gift. I've been waiting a long time to share it with people who I knew would care."

"What gift?" Ridley asked, annoyed. But then it came to her. Mr. Vernon's letter. The *confession*.

Kalagan's laughter came like puffs of smoke from a locomotive's stack. "I imagine it was quite a surprise. Learning what your beloved Dante Vernon was up to all those years ago. How his jealousy, his rage, his self-ishness turned him into what some folks might call…a *monster*."

Leila's eyes shot wide. "My father is not—"

"Yes, yes." Kalagan waved her off. "We already know what you think your father is not. But I came here today to convince you of what he *is*. My question: Are you ready to listen? Or will you continue to cover your ears like one of those little monkeys in the famous illustration?"

"Don't talk about monkeys that way!" said Olly.

"Yeah," Izzy added. "Change-O is our friend."

Kalagan tilted his top hat as he glanced their way. *"Funny."* His voice came out like a purr. "I like you two. Annoying, but in a charming way."

"We're not annoying," Izzy said, looking hurt.

"I called you *charming*, my dear," Kalagan added. "Don't twist it up."

The way this man spoke was making Ridley disoriented and dizzy. His sentences felt like sharp arrows, shot confidently, wildly, and that might hit a bull's-eye if they let them.

"All of you have something to offer one another. Carter's endurance. Leila's enthusiasm. Theo's logic. Ridley's strength. I can understand why you six have stuck together so solidly over the past few months. You make a good team. And *that* is something to cherish. I long to have my old team back together again. My Emerald Ring. But Dante Vernon has worked hard to make sure that will never happen. Even after he admitted to *murdering* my parents."

Ridley gritted her teeth. "I'm very sorry about what happened to your parents," she said. "But after everything we've already seen you do here in Mineral Wells, how can we trust that you didn't write that letter yourself?"

"Show it to Dante. Watch his reaction. I have a feeling that you already have your doubts about him. The man has his secrets, doesn't he?"

Carter and Leila glanced at each other with worry. Ridley remembered how important it had been to Leila to get her dad to open up over the summer. And he'd still kept things from them. Was Kalagan correct? Were there things that Mr. Vernon didn't want them to know about himself because they were too dark? Too horrible? Too dangerous?

"I know that what I'm saying is resonating in your hearts, like the strings of Theo's violin as he brings his bow magically across them. I am not a bad person. No worse than your beloved mentor. I am only trying to show you what is real. And what is a trick."

"What do you want from us?" Theo asked.

"I want you to convince Dante Vernon to join my new...*club*. If he were to come over to my side, he would bring all of the talent of his own Magic Circle with him."

"Those were the names he had hidden in his ledger. The names you tried to get Sandra Santos to steal for you," said Leila.

Kalagan shrugged, as if the attempted theft had been no big deal. "Together, we shall do wonders. We will all live as we were meant to. You, Dante, me. And every magician who cares to join us. We will be unstoppable."

Ridley glanced at her friends. Each of them looked exhausted. There was something appealing about the idea of surrender. Wasn't there? To be part of a group that wasn't fighting all the time? To have a charismatic leader, who had a clear vision of what he imagined was best for everyone? Ridley saw a bit of herself in Kalagan's argument. She often thought that she was right. And she wanted her friends to fall in line behind her.

But...

She also knew that that bit of herself was one of the pieces she most wanted to change. No one likes being told what to do all the time. Especially not by a single person with a very loud voice.

"No," Ridley heard herself say.

"Excuse me?" asked Kalagan, raising his hand to the brim of his hat.

"No," Leila answered this time.

"No," said Carter and Theo and Olly and Izzy.

"*No*," Kalagan echoed, his voice distorted by the cave's acoustics. He nodded slowly as he brought his hand away from his top hat. A black wand with white tips appeared at his fingers. He wiggled it at them, and it seemed to glint, transforming into a blade briefly before changing back into a wand. "I must admit, Misfits, that I'm disappointed. But I see now that Vernon reached you earlier than I ever could have. He's gotten inside your heads. Mesmerized you into following him."

"That's *your* deal, Kalagan," said Ridley. "Not Mr. Vernon's."

"Of course you'd believe that," he whispered, sounding disappointed. Kalagan held his wand over his hat and then flicked it slightly toward them. The large man and woman who had accompanied him down the path from the woods stepped forward. "Thankfully, I came prepared with a backup plan. You all shall come with me now. And if Dante wants you back, he'll turn over the names of the Magic Circle, whether he likes it or not." Kalagan pointed his wand at the group and whispered, "Get them."

"Help!" Leila called out. "Dad! Poppa! Somebody!"

The goons came forward, completely blocking the mouth of the cave. Ridley knew the trio wouldn't be able to catch hold of all of her friends, but if they managed to grab only one, that would be enough.

She shot back to the magic box. The other Misfits steadied themselves, raising their magical weapons. Ridley turned a crank near the bottom of the box, and it began to tilt rapidly backward toward the track. As the box slammed down, its wheels connected with the rails.

Carter dashed in front of Kalagan, zipping his slippery cards at the man's feet, but Kalagan hopped over them easily. Leila flung a loop of rope at one of the burly goons, but he ducked out of the way.

Ridley pulled a cord at the side of the box, and the

lid dropped off and clattered to the ground. Now the magic box looked like a railway car or a mine cart, open at the top with just enough room for the Misfits to fit inside.

"Stop her!" Kalagan shouted.

The Misfits finally noticed what Ridley was doing, and they gaped for a moment at the magic box's transformation.

"Careful!" Ridley called out as Kalagan's goons flanked Olly and Izzy. The twins backflipped across a boulder and landed near Ridley's cart. "Get in," she told them, and they cartwheeled up and over the edge.

The goons caught sight of Leila and bolted toward her instead. Leila ran toward the edge of the cave and pressed her back against the rock. When the goons got close, Leila ducked down and slid between them. When they tried to turn, they found that their shoelaces were tied in a loose bow, which was enough to bring them down. Leila skipped toward the magic box and scooted in behind Olly and Izzy.

"Stand up, you fools!" Kalagan shouted at the goons, who were now rolling on the ground, trying to yank their shoes off.

Ridley pulled a lever, which released a small plank

at the rear of her magic box. She backed herself up and perched on the platform, snapping two metal clasps across her tires, locking her wheels in place.

Theo had dashed to the other side of the cave's mouth and was close to the gravel path that led up the slope to the resort. He turned and saw Kalagan spread his cloak out as he descended on Carter. Theo brought his bow across the strings of his violin, releasing a shriek that bounced off the rocks and rattled everyone's ears. It was enough to make Kalagan miss his mark; his arms closed upon nothing as Carter ducked. But before he could dash to safety, Carter tripped, landing on his back and looking up at the man in the top hat.

"Oh no!" Leila cried, about to hop out of the cart to help him.

"Wait, Leila!" Theo shouted. He made his violin and bow disappear into his jacket and then leapt from boulder to boulder until he was close enough to barrel into Kalagan's side. The man stumbled as Theo grabbed Carter's hand and yanked him to his feet. Carter threw down a small pellet that burst into a cloud of thick black smoke, and the two boys raced toward the magic box cart.

Kalagan was nowhere to be seen.

"What *is* this thing?" Theo asked, out of breath, hopping into the box. There was just enough space left over for Carter to follow.

"Our escape," said Ridley, reaching down and pushing a lever near the rails. The box shuddered and began to roll farther into the cave.

"Where are we going?" Leila yelped.

"Mr. Vernon says a good magician always plans for an out," Ridley answered. "And this is ours!" The box began to pick up speed, and the blot of daylight at the mouth of the cave started to shrink.

"Where's Kalagan?" Carter asked. Ridley looked around, but the smoke that Carter had released was obscuring the shadows.

Just then, voices called out to them from up the hill. Glancing into the sunlight, Ridley could see four figures approaching quickly. They were running down the path, as if to try to catch the Misfits before they could get away. Ridley recognized a couple of them. There was Quinn, the concierge from the lobby of the Grand Oak. Her blond ponytail bobbed behind her as she jogged. She was followed by a man and a woman dressed in hotel uniforms, the people who had been speaking with the twins the other night—Mrs. Golden's dance assistant and Izzy's singing teacher. On their heels was an elderly woman that Ridley had never seen before. Her head spun as the cart moved faster into the cave. Kalagan's mesmerism victims were everywhere! How many people were under his spell?

A shape leapt out of the shadows at the back of the cart. White gloved hands grabbed Ridley's footrests. She screamed. Kalagan had recovered. His goons appeared out of the smoke beside him. Kalagan's top hat bounced as he struggled to keep up. The goons ran quickly too, grappling with the sides of the cart. They groaned as they dug their heels into the dirt and threw their weight backward. The cart slowed dramatically, and the Misfits all yelped.

(Oh, dear reader! Now you know why I felt so anxious at the beginning of this adventure! Are our Misfits goners??)

But Ridley had one trick left up her sleeve.

She reached her hand backward and slammed her palm against a big red button on the bottom of what had once been her magic box, releasing a spring-loaded gear that she had originally designed for the inventors' fair last weekend.

There was a squealing sound as the cart's wheels spun rapidly against the rails. The goons lost their grip, and Kalagan was forced to let go of Ridley's foot-rests, as the Misfits were carried at full tilt into the depths of the ice cave.

TWENTY

Darkness enveloped them. Ridley felt the tracks slant, and the cart sped up even more. Wind caught her curls, whipping them in front of her face. Clacking noises echoed as the wheels met rust and decay along the rails. Ridley sucked her teeth every time the vehicle jerked, praying that both the tracks and the wheels would hold.

Her friends were shouting. The track dipped and they shot down like a rocket, before gravity pulled at them and they swung back up a slight hill.

"Where are we going?" Theo yelled.

"I can't see anything!" Leila yelled back.

Carter was strangely quiet, but maybe—Ridley considered—this was how he dealt with being terrified.

"Wheeee!" shrieked the twins.

The magic box cart raced deeper into the earth. Ridley flipped the light switch at the arm of her chair, the thin beam glowing back up the track from where they'd come. The track curved tightly, and their bodies were slammed to one side.

Ridley felt the cart begin to tilt. "Lean!" she called out. "To the other side! Lean!"

The wheels reconnected with the rails, and Ridley heaved a sigh. But then, the track sloped down again and the cart raced faster than ever. Would it never end? Ridley had assumed they'd find a quick exit, and yet the darkness kept speeding by. The small light from Ridley's chair flashed across the mouths of deep crevices where icy air blasted out like the breath of a long-frozen beast.

(All right, I know what you're thinking. It seems a bit improbable that the Misfits haven't flown right off

the rails into a rock-filled crevice by now. That said, we're having a great ride, aren't we? So quit thinking about it and hold on tight!)

There was a rushing sound ahead that grew louder as the tracks sloped steeper and steeper. A strange light began to fill the tunnel. Cold. Blue. Ridley craned her neck to get a glimpse of where they were headed. Mist and spray clung to her eyelashes and eyebrows. A hazy glow was widening at the bottom of the slope. The Misfits' cries were not enough to drown out the sound of pounding water.

Ridley bit her lip, hoping she hadn't sent them all to meet their final fates. She wanted to call out to them, to apologize. To tell them she loved them. But the cart bottomed out, slamming her jaw shut, and then shot upward. The magic box left the track altogether, flying off a sudden ragged edge and into the curtain of spray at the end of the tunnel.

A frozen sensation coated Ridley's body, plastering her hair to her skull. Water filled her mouth and went up her nose. She felt weightless, and for a moment, she couldn't tell if she was soaring or sinking. Then, without warning, the cart crashed down, knocking Ridley's chin nearly against her chest. Water splashed out in a high, wide fan all around the magic box cart as it landed over a dozen yards out from the cliff at the edge of a lake.

It took several seconds for Ridley to feel like she was inside her body again, and when she did, she gulped down a huge lungful of air. The blue sky overhead was blindingly bright. Shaking her hair from her face, she called out to her friends, "Is everyone okay?" From behind her came groans.

"I think so," said Leila.

"Define okay," Theo answered.

"That was awesome!" chirped Izzy.

"Can we ride it again?" Olly added.

"What about you, Carter?" Ridley asked.

"Fine," he said with such curtness that everyone knew he was not *fine* at all.

Ridley glanced down and noticed that water had already crept up to the bottom of the footrest on her chair. The magic box cart was sinking!

Thankfully, Ridley had a plan for that....

She grabbed the handle of yet another lever at the bottom of the box and gave it a yank. The sides of the box popped off, transforming it into a raft. "Don't let those panels float away," she called to her friends.

"We can use them as oars to get ourselves back to shore."

The others all looked at her in amazement.

"Guys! Grab the panels!" Ridley urged. "This thing is going to sink fast."

Olly and Izzy snatched up the panels and began propelling the raft forward. Luckily they were already drifting closer to their destination thanks to the momentum from their wild ride through the tunnels.

"Ridley Larsen!" Leila exclaimed. "*How* did you build this thing?"

Ridley sniffed. She was surprised that all the buttons, levers, and transformations had worked so well. Looking back toward the misty falls, she couldn't believe that they had actually survived the short flight over the jagged rocks at the bottom of the cliff. It felt like a magic trick, possibly the grandest one ever performed!

"Very carefully," Ridley answered.

Olly laughed giddily as he pulled at the water with his oar panel.

"I'm not trying to be funny. I *very carefully* planned it all out, then *very carefully* put it together. It took weeks and weeks."

"It is, without a doubt, your greatest invention," Theo agreed.

"I can't believe you anticipated every problem we might encounter," Leila said, shaking her head in amazement.

"Whoa," said Izzy, using the other oar panel to steer the boat toward the houses settled on the far shore of the lake. "You're an *actual* genius, Ridley."

Ridley's skin warmed. Her instinct was to blurt out something rude to change the subject and take the focus off herself. "Thanks, Izzy," she said with a smile instead. "Thanks, all. I'm just glad it worked."

As they reached an empty beach made of multi-colored pebbles (and just in time, I might add), Ridley turned around to catch a glimpse of her friends stumbling off the raft. As she unhooked herself from the back, she noticed Carter had not moved. He sat at the front, hanging his head.

"Carter?" Ridley asked. "You okay?"

"I saw something," he said. "Back at the cave entrance."

"We all saw lots of things," said Leila. "But we made it out of there. We're safe now."

"We're *not* safe," said Carter. "We'll never be safe.

Not until we stop him." The others were quiet, not knowing how to comfort him. Ridley had never seen Carter so despondent. "I saw his face," Carter added with a whisper. "I know who he is."

"You saw Kalagan?" Izzy asked.

"We already know who he is," said Olly. "He's *Kalagan*!"

Carter shivered, plucking his wet shirt and jacket away from his torso. "The man in the cave...in the top hat and the cape...The man who threatened us...who has been tormenting us for months...His face...it was my uncle Sly."

"Wait," said Leila. "What?"

Cogs turned in Ridley's mind as little events and coincidences started to fit together. She maneuvered her chair out of the shallow water and onto dry land so she could think better.

"When the man in the top hat crouched over me, his collar slipped. I saw his eyes. I would recognize them anywhere. They were the eyes that glared at me when I was little and wouldn't or couldn't do what my uncle asked. They were the eyes that went dull and blank whenever I made a suggestion about where to stay, what to eat, or how to live. They were the eyes that were filled with glee when they saw how fast I could shuffle a deck of cards. Those eyes, that face...how could I ever forget it?" His shoulders began to heave, and he covered his own face as he cried.

"Oh, Carter!" said Leila. "There's got to be some sort of explanation."

"What if the explanation is that Kalagan has been masquerading as Carter's long-lost relative for Carter's entire life?" said Ridley. Leila widened her eyes, pleading silently for Ridley to be sensitive. But there were times for sensitivity, and then there were times to make everyone see clearly. "It makes sense. All of our troubles with Kalagan started when Carter came to Mineral Wells."

Carter whipped his head around, red streaks running down his cheeks. "This is not my fault!"

"That's not what I meant!" Ridley retorted. "We know that Kalagan's plans have centered on Mr. Vernon. And getting the names of Vernon's magic club. What I'm saying...what we already know...is that Kalagan can manipulate people. What if, Carter—what if that night you ran away from him...what if that's what he *wanted* you to do?" Carter shook his head in disbelief. "What if he chased you through that train yard so you'd end up hopping onto one train in particular? One that would terminate here in Mineral Wells?" Now Carter's eyes glazed over as if he were looking inward, remembering. "What if he made sure you would find Mr. Vernon? And the magic shop? And us?"

"How?" asked Leila. "How could Kalagan do *all that*?"

Ridley shrugged. "People have been telling us for months how terrifying his power is. What if what we've seen him do here in Mineral Wells has only been the tip of the iceberg?"

"Iceberg?" Olly said, glancing out at the water they'd just traveled through. "Where?"

"Not now, Olly," Izzy chastised him quietly.

"He had access to your dad's puzzle box, Carter. He could have slipped Vernon's confession letter inside at any time while you were still together, then scattered the other boxes here in Mineral Wells, so that we'd find them exactly when he wanted us to."

"Why now?" asked Theo.

"Because he's used up all his other options," Ridley finished. "He needed us to go through everything with Bosso and Sandra and Vernon and the magic shop so that we'd understand where he's coming from. He needed us to see that Vernon can be shifty and secretive and just as manipulative as he is."

Leila crunched her brow. "My father is not—"

But Ridley cut her off. "It doesn't matter what your father is or isn't, Leila. Kalagan's plan worked." She swallowed a nothingness down her dry throat. "It worked on *me*. I don't know about the rest of you, but I have doubt. Deep down, I wonder about Mr. Vernon's real intentions." The magic box raft began to drift down the pebbly beach, but no one moved to stop it.

"*You* have doubt," Leila said, her voice trembling. "But *I* don't. And I never will."

Theo stood. "Okay, okay. We need to keep moving. I do not believe it is a good idea for us to be out on our own. Ridley's house is closest. Can we go there to dry off?"

"My dads need to know what's going on," said Leila. "We should have told them much earlier than now." She scowled at Ridley.

Ridley tried to let it fall away like water off an oil-cloth sack, but it wasn't working.

(When speaking a hard truth, like Ridley had just done, you must be prepared to have the reaction of others soak through your clothes, then your skin, then get into your bones.)

They left the magic box raft on the shore and made their way up to the line of trees. It was difficult to move through the maze of saplings and knotted-up roots after everything they'd just been through, but eventually, the group spilled out onto the street at the far edge of Ridley's neighborhood. They headed up the center of the road, fearful that any of Kalagan's mesmerized hoodlums could come out from around a hedge or a car and catch them. Leila and Theo held Carter's hands as Ridley followed with Olly and Izzy on either side.

"What I don't understand is how my uncle could have been in so many places at once," Carter said. "I mean, yeah, there were a few nights here and there when he wouldn't come back to the rooms where we boarded. But those were rare. If he really planned out everything we *think* he did, he wouldn't have had time to teach me all those magic tricks. Or spend so much time pretending to be a small-time con artist. It feels like what he did is impossible. Unless—" He stopped suddenly. Ridley almost plowed into him. "Unless... magic *is* real?" he added quietly.

"Oh, Carter," Leila said. "There's nothing magical about that man."

"He was working with someone," said Ridley. *"Obviously."*

"Yeah," said Olly. "Bosso and Sandra and his frown clown friends."

"Ooh-ooh!" Izzy raised her hand, as if she were in a classroom and wanted to be called on. "And... Quinn. And my mom's dance assistant and my singing instructor. They were at the mouth of the cave just after Kalagan showed up. *They* were trying to help him catch us too."

Ridley thought of her teacher and wondered how she fit into the mess that was the mesmerist, the mesmerized mafia, and the manipulated.

"When we get to Ridley's house, we'll call my dads," said Leila again.

"Maybe we should hold off on that for just a bit," said Ridley, still feeling that *doubt* she'd mentioned a few minutes earlier.

"*Really?*" Leila looked like she wanted to explode. Carter stayed silent and walked on.

To Ridley's surprise, Theo stood up for her. "All we need right now is a place to hide. We can figure out the rest once we are safe and sound."

Safe and sound. The words seemed to hang in the air, all shimmery, before falling like glass to the ground. Ridley hadn't said anything to her friends when they suggested her house, but with all the work she needed to get done, would Mrs. Larsen even let her friends *inside*?

As the group came around the corner, and Ridley's house appeared, Ridley saw that the mint-green Plymouth was not parked in the driveway. *That's right!* Ridley remembered. *Mom said she had an appointment this afternoon.*

Relieved, she opened the door for her friends and waited as they passed into the foyer. But before she could slip inside with them, a voice shouted from behind her. "Ridley, wait!" Footsteps creaked swiftly up the front steps.

Ridley spun her chair to face whoever it was, ready to blast them with water or sound or even electricity. Ms. Parkly saw Ridley's poised fingers, and then raised her own hands. The world went dizzy. It was Saturday.

They didn't have any lessons scheduled. So then why was Ms. Parkly here?

"I heard about what happened," said the teacher, glancing over her shoulder. "Quick, get inside."

"What do you mean?" Ridley gripped the wheels of her chair. "*What* happened?"

"Ridley, we don't have time for this. They're coming for us. Get. Inside. *Now.*"

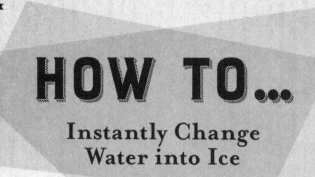

HOW TO...

Instantly Change Water into Ice

I don't know about you, but I'm still shivering after that dunk the Misfits took in the lake. Or perhaps it has something to do with our next lesson, which allows you to change a cup of water into cubes of ice before your audience's very eyes. Brrr! You might want to put a sweater on for this one.

WHAT YOU'LL NEED:

A plastic cup (Make sure it's not clear, or the trick will be revealed.)

A drinking glass with a small amount of water inside

A sponge

3 or 4 ice cubes

TO PREPARE:

Shove the sponge into the bottom of the opaque cup.

Place the ice cubes in the cup, on top of the sponge.

HELPFUL HINT:

Make sure not to tilt the cup toward the audience. You don't want to give away the secret!

STEPS:

1. Present the glass of water to the audience and tell them you're going to change the water's color. (This part is a fib, but that's okay, because it will only make the trick more surprising later on.)

2. Pour the water from the drinking glass into the opaque cup. (The sponge will soak up the small amount of water.)

3. Wave your hand over the top of the opaque cup and say some magic words. (I'm sure by now you have a few up your sleeve.)

4. Then pour the "water" back into the drinking glass.

CLINK CLINK

5. When the ice cubes clink into the glass, act as surprised as the audience. Try saying "Oopsie!" It usually gets a laugh. Dad jokes work too. Try "Do my ICE deceive me?" Or "Man, that trick is COOL."

6. Give a wink and take a bow!

TWENTY-ONE

Ridley wouldn't budge. "Tell me what's going on," she said to Ms. Parkly. She felt movement in the doorway behind her. The Magic Misfits had her back.

Ms. Parkly shook her head. She seemed to be standing straighter, more confidently. There was no giggle or singsong to her deadly serious voice. "I'm here to help."

Ridley clutched the arms of her chair. "What's. Going. On?"

"Not out here!" But when Ridley still refused to move, Ms. Parkly's answer came out in a rush. "I know

★ 234 ★

what happened up at the ice cave. With Dean and that box. And *Kalagan*. Quinn, Gregor, and Tara saw you disappear down the tracks. You were so foolish to do something like that without consulting Dante! What were you thinking? We all worried that you were...but you're not! You're here. And you must let me in! I'm on your side."

When Ridley continued to glare at her, Ms. Parkly sighed. She plucked a leaf from one of the rhododendron plants growing up around the Larsens' front porch. Cupping it in her palms, she held it out to Ridley. "Go on, take it." Against her better judgment, Ridley reached out and lifted the leaf from her teacher's hands—only somehow it was no longer a leaf. A bright pink blossom dangled from Ridley's pinched fingertips.

Her eyebrows raised up, as if on their own. A bunch of gasps wafted out of the foyer behind her. Ridley started to ask, "How did you..."

Ms. Parkly rolled her eyes. "Oh boy, you're going to make me say it? Fine. Ridley Larsen, I am part of Mr. Vernon's Magic Circle. Under his request, I have been watching you, *guarding* you, since the end of the summer." She glanced over her shoulder at the seemingly quiet street. "The longer we stand out here, the more likely it is that one of the mesmerized will spot us. I'll explain everything if you let me in. I promise."

"Why should I trust you? After everything that's happened today?"

"You're right." Ms. Parkly looked beyond Ridley to the others. "Leila, I know you always carry a pair of thumb-cuffs. Toss them over. I'll put them on."

Stunned, Leila reached into her pants pocket and brought out the cuffs—big enough only to fit between the first and second knuckle of a pair of thumbs. She tossed them to Ridley's teacher, who immediately clicked them into place. Holding up her hands to show the group, she said, "Good enough?"

Ridley looked to her friends. She knew they didn't always agree, but right now, they all wore the same expression—one that said to let Ms. Parkly into the house. "All right. But we're watching you."

"Understood," Ms. Parkly replied, not tripping even slightly as they entered the foyer.

A few minutes later, they were seated around the living room, fresh towels draped across the furniture so that the Misfits' damp clothes wouldn't ruin Mrs. Larsen's expensive fabrics. Ms. Parkly perched in the middle of the couch and everyone listened as she explained. "I know that Dante can be less than forthcoming. And it must be frustrating to be kept in the dark. But he has his reasons. When he left Mineral Wells in August, it wasn't only because he'd gotten news that the Magic Circle had been compromised. He was also gathering together a group of the most trustworthy members of our club to come home with him, to live in secret among you, to watch you six and make sure that no harm came to you. We suspected that Kalagan would continue to target you. It turned out we were right."

Theo shook his head. "You mean...*each* of us has a secret guardian?"

Ms. Parkly nodded. "Can you guess who they are?"

Izzy gasped. "Gregor and Tara?"

"One for you and one for Olly," said Ms. Parkly.

"They were at the mouth of the cave to help us?" said Olly.

"But they weren't alone," said Leila. "Quinn the concierge was with them. Along with another person. Someone I didn't recognize."

"Quinn has long been a secret member of Dante's society. Since she was already in town, she agreed to keep an eye on Carter."

"Quinn?" Carter blurted out. "Watching me? I didn't even notice. And I usually notice."

"Who is the other person?" Leila asked. "The one who is watching me?"

"She's been staying at the hotel as a guest," said Ms. Parkly. "Keeping a low profile."

"And me?" Theo asked.

Ms. Parkly smiled. "You know how often you visit the pet store to pick up food for your doves?"

"Of course," said Theo. "*Quite* often."

"The clerk who sells you that food is a member of the Circle."

Theo nodded slowly, as if it were all coming together in his mind. "I *thought* it was strange how many questions he always asks about my birds."

Ms. Parkly raised her chin. "None of you realize that you'd met me before, do you?"

Ridley flinched. "Met you where? When?"

"At the beginning of the summer. I was doing some work for Dante, looking into B. B. Bosso's shady operations at the Mineral Wells fairgrounds. I was going by a different name then."

Carter's jaw dropped, his lips making a popping sound. "Madame Helga?"

Ms. Parkly let out the smallest of laughs, though nothing like the high-pitched one Ridley was used to. "The one and only."

"Wait, who?" asked Olly.

"You and Izzy weren't there," said Leila. "Madame Helga was the one who gave us our motto! *Alone we are weak. Together we are strong.*" She paused, then asked, "You're not really psychic, are you?"

"About as psychic as Sandra Santos," Ms. Parkly replied. "What you need to know most right now is that Dante Vernon cares greatly about *all* of you. What happened today at the ice caves was the result of several missteps. And for that, I apologize."

Ridley squinted at her teacher. She wanted to ask if the missteps were *actual* missteps, or if maybe, the missteps had occurred on purpose.

Something knocked at the window. Ridley saw a bright green parrot staring in through the newly replaced glass. "Presto!" Leila exclaimed, leaping to her feet. The bird blinked at the group and then tapped the glass with her beak again. Leila unlocked the window and slid the sash up. Presto flew inside and landed on her shoulder. "What are you doing here?"

"Talking to mesmerist. Too big. Too mega. Dogma

is phenomena worship," said the bird. "Talking to mesmerist. Too big. Too mega. Dogma is phenomena worship."

"She's doing that weird thing again," Izzy whispered to Olly.

"Don't let her hear you calling her *weird*," Olly whispered back. "Birds are sensitive."

Ms. Parkly leaned toward the side table next to the couch and reached for the drawer. She noticed Ridley stiffen, and then explained. "I need a paper and pen. Dante must have sent Presto to deliver a message to us."

Carter flinched. "What kind of a message is '*Talking to mesmerist. Too big. Too mega. Dogma is phenomena worship*'?"

"A *secret* message," said Ms. Parkly. "One that needs to be deciphered."

"Hold on," said Leila. "My *parrot* has been *speaking in code* this entire time and *I never knew it*?"

Ms. Parkly nodded, smirking, as if proud of the little bird.

Ridley rolled her eyes and sighed. "One more thing he's been keeping from us." She opened the panel in the arm of her chair, brought out a piece of paper and pen, and handed them to her teacher.

"To Dante's credit," said Ms. Parkly, "a secret society does need to keep *some* secrets. Now...what was it that the bird said again?"

"Talking to mesmerist. Too big. Too mega. Dogma is phenomena worship," Theo replied.

Presto glanced at him pleasantly.

Ms. Parkly wrote out the message on the page and showed it to the group. Then she circled the last letter in each word. When she rewrote each of the circled letters onto a new line at the bottom of the paper, Presto's secret message from Mr. Vernon was revealed: *Go to GOA ASAP.*

"GOA?" said Izzy. "What's a GOA?"

"And what's an ASAP?" asked Olly. "Are these even *more* code words?"

"GOA would be Grand Oak...Auditorium?" said Carter.

"And ASAP stands for As Soon As Possible," Theo added.

"Talking to mesmerist. Too big. Too mega. Dogma is phenomena worship," Presto said again.

Ms. Parkly went on. "There's a trick to it. You've got to say, 'What a fantastical bird!' After that, she'll repeat whatever you say next. To make her stop, you say the same words. 'What a fantastical bird!'" Presto stared at the teacher but did not speak again. "See? It worked!"

Presto perked up and said, "See? It worked!"

Ms. Parkly laughed. "What a fantastical bird!"

"I've definitely heard my dad say those words before." Leila clicked her tongue, and Presto nuzzled her nose. "If we get out of this mess, we are *so* playing around with this trick," she told the parrot.

"Why couldn't Mr. Vernon just call us on the phone?" asked Izzy.

"You never know who might be listening in. Depending on whether or not Kalagan had gotten to them, they might pass along whatever they heard."

"My dad wants us with him up at the resort," said Leila. "We should leave now." Carter stood.

"Wait," Ridley heard herself say. Everyone glanced at her. She felt heat in her chest. "Are we sure that's the right thing to do?"

"Of course it is," said Leila. "My dads will protect us."

Ridley thought about the confession letter, about all the things that Kalagan had told them of Mr. Vernon. Yes, Kilroy Kalagan was a jerk of the largest order, but that didn't mean all was fine with Vernon, who, everyone had to admit, had made some very, very big mistakes.

Theo stood beside Ridley and rested his hand on her shoulder. His expression told her that he was on her side. But then Ridley thought: The whole idea of *sides* meant that there was a split in the group. And hadn't Ms. Parkly—or Madame Helga at the time—told them that *together they were strong*? Her advice had gotten the Magic Misfits through so much. At this point, those words felt almost sacred.

Maybe Ridley and her friends would never agree completely about everything. Maybe that was fine. However, the issue of who was right about Mr. Vernon was one that Ridley knew had the power to split apart the Magic Misfits forever. Just what Kalagan wanted.

People so often say they can *agree to disagree*, but what if Ridley decided, for once, to *agree to agree*? What was her other option? Locking herself in her lab and hoping for the best? No. If Ridley had a choice here—and she *did* have a choice—she would choose her friends.

She would choose her first guardian.

She would choose Dante Vernon.

Ridley touched Theo's hand on her shoulder. Looking up at him, she nodded and said, "Let's go with them. Every one of us. Together."

TWENTY-TWO

Ms. Parkly led the group to the resort's trolley stop in the village. Despite the danger of being spotted by one of the people whom Kalagan was manipulating, the trolley was the only way for them to travel to the Grand Oak together, which they all agreed was the safest way to go.

It was late afternoon when they arrived, the sun shifting behind the trees on the hill, casting weblike shadows across the resort's wide front lawn. No staff member greeted them at the entrance. They opened the doors themselves and crept through the lobby, all the way to the back hall, which snaked around toward the auditorium.

The day had been long, and Ridley's arms ached as she maneuvered her chair along the pathway. Her brain ached too. So much had happened. Way too much to process. If the Misfits managed to get themselves out of this situation, Ridley knew it would take at least a week of tinkering in her lab to calm her down again. But at least she'd have her friends to keep her company.

"Wait here," Ms. Parkly whispered as the Misfits came into the starkly empty lobby of the auditorium. She approached one door of the theater and then sounded a peculiar knock. Ridley figured it must be another type of code—something that Vernon's Magic Circle had agreed upon—because next, there was the click of a lock being undone and the door creaked open wide. It looked dark inside the theater, with only the single bulb of a ghost light standing upon the stage. Ridley could see figures moving in the murk.

Then she heard a familiar voice. "Friends!" Mr. Vernon's face appeared to slide out of the shadows as he stepped into the lobby light.

"Dad!" Leila cheered.

"Dante!" Carter cried out.

They both ran to embrace the tall man with the curly white mop of hair who was dressed, as usual, in a sharp black tuxedo and cape lined with red silk.

Ridley knew he was the same man she had adored for years, but somehow he looked different. She wished that Kalagan had kept the stupid secret awful letter to himself.

(But that's the thing about revenge—its blast radius is wide and usually circles more than only the intended target. Take my advice: Leave *revenging* to characters in Westerns and samurai movies, where it belongs!)

Ridley felt Theo and the twins sidle up behind her, just as Mr. Vernon glanced out at them. He held his arms aloft, as if he had the power to bring them closer to him. It seemed to work, because soon, all of the Misfits were huddled around the magician. "I'm so glad you're all here, that you're all safe. Is everyone okay? How did you travel here?" he asked. They all started to talk at once, to assure their older friend that they were strong and brave and ready. Ridley thought to herself: *Yeah, but we're still only a bunch of kids. We shouldn't have to be all of those things. Not yet.*

"Where's Poppa?" Leila asked, peering into the darkness behind Mr. Vernon.

"Here I am, honey," came a warm voice from the shadows. The Other Mr. Vernon waved. Leila raced ahead and threw her arms around his soft middle. His big arms nearly encompassed her entire head. "Come in, all of you," said the Other Mr. Vernon. "Quickly. And lock that door, Helena, please." Ms. Parkly did as he asked, and then followed the group into the auditorium.

Ridley eased her chair down the aisle, past the many rows of seats, closer to the glow of that single bulb shining from the otherwise pitch-black stage. When everyone reached the front row, they gathered together as if around a campfire. The Other Mr. Vernon revealed a tray filled with freshly baked chocolate chip cookies and passed it around the group. As Ridley grabbed two of the biggest cookies, she realized how hungry she actually was. Her mother was probably home from her appointment by now and might have started making dinner. Ridley wished that she had remembered to leave a note. Her mother might not have seen it, or if so, she might not have read it, but Ridley imagined it to be something that an ordinary daughter would have done for an ordinary mother.

Mr. Vernon stood before them. "By now, I imagine that Ms. Parkly has likely told you about your guardians." The Misfits whispered affirmatively. "I'm sorry for once again keeping you all in the dark, but I figured the less you knew about my friends who were keeping you safe, the safer you all would be."

"We're sorry too," said Leila. "We didn't tell you the whole truth either. That's why Kalagan ended up coming for us in the cave."

Mr. Vernon smiled kindly. "You can tell us now," he suggested. The Other Mr. Vernon put down the tray of cookies and took his husband's hand.

"We have *lots* to tell you," said Ridley, making sure it was clear to everyone that despite her misgivings, she had chosen to trust their mentor. "Maybe Carter can start?"

Carter shuddered. He told the Vernons about Kalagan's alter ego as his uncle, Sylvester Beaton.

Of course, the Vernons had questions galore. When everyone had said what they'd wanted to say about it, Ridley knew it was time to get to the heart of the matter. Retrieving the taped-together confession letter from the compartment in the arm of her chair, she spoke up before her nerves could take hold. "Mr. Vernon, we need to show you something." He looked quizzically at the page in her hand.

"What's that, Ridley?"

"A letter that you wrote a long time ago. A letter to your old friend, Kilroy Kalagan." She saw Mr. Vernon's face grow pale, and she glanced at the others, none of whom could meet her eye. Or Mr. Vernon's. She considered reading it out loud, but then figured maybe the Other Mr. Vernon didn't need to hear the letter's contents, so she just handed it over.

The paper crinkled loudly in Mr. Vernon's grip. He squinted to read the old words written in his own handwriting. As he scanned to the bottom of the page, his eyes grew wider, and then he shook his head. He glanced at the Misfits and sniffed. "Let me guess," he said. "Kalagan made sure this ended up in your hands."

"He sure did make sure," Ridley said with a nod. "In *all* of our hands. He put one piece into each of the old Emerald Ring puzzle boxes. We opened them the other night. We weren't sure we should show you immediately. We wanted to get more information from Dean."

"A very unwise move, Ridley," said Mr. Vernon with concern. He glanced at each of the Misfits. "You all could have gotten seriously hurt. What were you thinking?"

"We were thinking we couldn't trust you!" Ridley's voice echoed throughout the auditorium, just like it had at the cave earlier that day.

Mr. Vernon winced as if she'd slapped him. He was quiet for a moment. "And are you *still* thinking that?" he asked.

Ridley held out her hand, nervously indicating the letter. "What do you expect us to think? We want to trust you. Of course we do. But it seems you're always keeping something from us, and this is the biggest *something* yet."

The Other Mr. Vernon interrupted. "Is anyone going to tell me what's happening here?" Mr. Vernon gently put the page into his husband's palm, and the Other Mr. Vernon began to read.

Mr. Vernon turned back to Ridley. "This was an apology letter."

"An apology for causing someone's parents *to die*," Ridley came back, her voice on the verge of breaking. "For causing your friend Mick to be horribly burned."

"So then, you *did* write the letter, Dad?" Leila asked quietly.

"I did. And I meant every word." Mr. Vernon let out a long breath. "I wish...everything had turned out differently. I wish I could go back in time. Make a different decision. But what's past is past."

The Other Mr. Vernon folded the paper and placed it on the stage behind him. Ms. Parkly stood off to the side and crossed her arms, looking uncomfortable. Ridley couldn't tell what either of them were thinking, but their silence told her it wasn't good. Had Kalagan achieved his goal of turning Dante Vernon into a villain? Had Ridley helped him?

"I'm sorry I never told you any of this," said Mr. Vernon. "I really am. But there are certain things that we feel such shame over, such fear, such anger, it's hard to not keep it secret." He faced his husband. "I made a horrible mistake. And I made another mistake when I kept it to myself."

"But you didn't keep it to yourself, Dante." The Other Mr. Vernon shook his head. "You apologized directly to the person who you hurt. *He* was the person who you were supposed to talk to. And that's what you did. How he responded was not up to you. To be honest, how he responded is *horrifying*." He held out his arms and then wrapped his husband in a tight embrace. Holding Dante, the Other Mr. Vernon went on. "I've always believed that a person's character is revealed in how he, she, or they face adversity. In my view, you have extraordinary character. You're a loving father. You're an attentive partner. You're a fighter. You're a *magician*. You want to share *wonder* with the world. How amazing and how pure! I would never let someone with a grudge try to steal that from you. Or from me. Or from them." He nodded toward the kids sitting in the front row. "I love you. And I know they do too."

Mr. Vernon whispered into the Other Mr. Vernon's ear. "Thank you, James. I'm so sorry."

Ridley felt her face burn with embarrassment. She glanced at Leila and Carter and saw them wiping tears from their eyes. Theo bit at his lip and picked at a fingernail. Olly and Izzy sat still, oddly quiet.

There was a knock at the auditorium door. It sounded just like the knock Ms. Parkly had given when they'd arrived. Mr. Vernon said, "Pardon me." Then he ran back up the aisle to let in whoever it was.

Ridley's mind buzzed. She knew she'd had to present the letter to Mr. Vernon, but now *she* felt like a villain. Whatever Kalagan had wanted to happen afterward, this had been the opposite. She tried to imagine her own parents talking about each other the way the Other Mr. Vernon talked about Dante, and she almost started laughing. Some people were good at sharing stuff like that. And other people...*weren't*.

But maybe that was okay too.

A group of people descended the aisle toward the stage. Ridley made out their faces in the glow of the ghost light. There were Quinn and Gregor and Tara. There was a man Ridley had seen working at the counter in the pet store where Theo bought his bird food.

One person trailed the others. Ridley didn't recognize this woman. She limped slowly with a cane. Her hair cascaded in front of her face in white wisps. Her hips filled out a long, dark dress. She must have been the hotel guest that Ms. Parkly had mentioned—the woman who had been Leila's guardian.

The group approached, led by a weary-looking Mr. Vernon. "Misfits, meet your guardians," he said. "Guardians, say hello to your Misfits."

As the adults went up to their respective kid, Helena Parkly came over to Ridley. "Are you all right?" she asked. "I imagine that was a really difficult thing to do."

Ridley shook her head. She wanted to appear strong and brave and a little bit mean, as usual. But she also wanted to be honest. She went with honest. "It *was* hard." The tears finally came. She wiped angrily at her eyes. "Sometimes I just feel like none of the grown-ups in my life are quite who I want them to be."

"That can't feel good. But please know that this is what Kalagan wants you to feel," said Ms. Parkly. "That's part of his plan. It's what he feeds off. Like an emotional vampire. Distrust, sadness, anger, and fear make him thrive."

"I know that. I know he's a bad guy. But...I feel like a bad guy myself."

"We *all* do sometimes," said Ms. Parkly. "A big part of growing up is learning how to forgive yourself. It's what Dante had to do when Kilroy Kalagan refused to accept any kind of apology."

Leila let out a shriek. Ridley spun her chair, ready to fight, but she saw that Leila wasn't in any trouble. She was, however, staring up at her guardian, who was

holding a white wig in her hands. The hotel guest's long dark hair was tucked into a tight black cap. She no longer needed her cane. And she appeared to have shed a few decades off her age, simply by standing up straighter. Then Ridley noticed the woman's large brown eyes. "Sandra," she whispered.

Ms. Parkly stood beside Ridley. "Speaking of forgiveness...*She* came to Dante's Magic Circle begging for mercy. They decided to give her another chance. And here she is. In disguise as Leila's guardian."

"I don't know how I feel about that," Ridley answered. "She betrayed us. She tried to hurt us."

"And now she's helping again. But you're allowed to feel what you feel, Ridley."

"Thank you, Ms. Parkly," Ridley said with a slight smile. She was so used to being told that her feelings of anger or frustration were wrong. She looked over to Leila and Sandra again and watched as her friend hugged their former enemy.

Something clicked into place in Ridley's head, like a lever and a latch attached to a new invention in her lab. Mr. Vernon had come to trust Sandra Santos again because she had asked him to. Despite all he had lost, he forgave her because she was sorry. And now Leila was doing the same. Could it be as easy as that?

There was more knocking at the auditorium door, and Ridley watched awestruck as dozens of people began to pour into the room. She recognized some of them from around town over the past few weeks. To her surprise, the people began to remove wigs and thick glasses and fake, oversized teeth.

They'd all been wearing disguises, just as Sandra had done. And as the Misfits had done...pretty badly.

"Who are they?" Ridley asked Ms. Parkly.

"Members of our magical society," she answered, pride beaming from her wide eyes. "The Circle. Mr. Vernon asked them to come and help. Safety in numbers."

Ridley thought of Presto the parrot flying around over Mineral Wells, screeching out Mr. Vernon's secret message far and wide about where to meet.

Speaking of Mr. Vernon, he suddenly looked a bit more energized, welcoming everyone, shaking hands, introducing his husband and the rest of the Misfits to whoever was standing closest.

Suddenly, there arose a different kind of knocking on the auditorium door. It came not only from the lobby area but also from backstage, near the service entrance where workers could load in theatrical sets.

The knocking became a pounding. The doors shook on their hinges. Worried, the Misfits looked to one another.

Soon, Ridley realized that this pounding was not coming from members of Vernon's Magic Circle asking to be let in.

Kalagan's mesmerized army had arrived.

TWENTY-THREE

A great booming sound rang out as the wood of the lobby doors split. Hands reached through the cracks like monsters in a scary movie. They pulled away the debris and tossed it aside.

Ridley backed up against the front edge of the stage near the orchestra pit. When her friends joined her, the guardians formed a barrier between them and the people who were clamoring through the now open doorway. Ridley recognized many citizens of Mineral Wells, whose eyes seemed glazed over, who were mouthing the words *What have I done?* The few faces that leapt out in particular were the librarian who had smashed her project the previous weekend, the cashier who Carter and Leila had confronted in the grocery store, and the two burly goons who had been Kalagan's guards in the ice cave that morning.

The crowd rushed down the aisle, leaping over rows of chairs, their chanting rising higher and higher. A cracking noise exploded from the back of the stage. Ridley saw that the doors there had been knocked down too, metal slabs lying crumpled on the floor. More of Kalagan's mesmerized followers came through, crowding onto the stage.

Ridley felt such panic, she didn't even think to pre-pare her chair's defenses. She reached out to Theo and to Leila.

"What's happening?" Leila asked. "What do they want?"

"This was always going to be Kalagan's endgame," Theo answered. "He wants to destroy everything Mr. Vernon holds dear. And he wants the Circle for him-self."

"I'm scared," Izzy whimpered.

"Hi, *Scared*," Olly answered. "I'm Olly." Izzy snick-ered and then clutched him tightly.

Mr. Vernon held a wand over his head. He let out a whoop and then called out his favorite magic words, "SIM SALA BIM!" When the mesmerized goons did not stop coming, he flicked his wrist, and a flurry of white sparks blossomed from the tip of the wand, pouring forth like fireworks on the Fourth of July. He leapt jauntily forward, bending one knee like a sword fighter, spewing sparks at the faces of the closest attackers.

The other members of the Circle responded with their own cry. "SIM SALA BIM!"

Ridley knew the call was merely misdirection, but still, the words felt powerful, as if they could release the mesmerized townspeople from their supposed spell.

The group of six guardians tightened around the Misfits, each of them raising fists or handbags or strings of costume jewelry as potential weapons. The rest of the Circle rushed at the citizens of Mineral Wells, igniting flash paper, dropping smoke pellets, swinging glowing-string lassos over their heads, blowing glitter bombs from palms, spraying water from bow ties, vanishing underneath cloaks, pulling billy clubs from out of wide top hats, revealing bunches of paper flowers, tying knots in shoelaces and necklaces, levitating, changing outfits with the snapping of fingers. It was all distraction, Ridley knew, to keep the intruders at bay and allow the rest of the group to get out of the line of attack.

Mr. Vernon appeared in front of the Misfits with the Other Mr. Vernon. "Follow us," he said. The six kids and six guardians raced around the orchestra pit to the side of the stage where a ramp curled up to the darkened wings.

The sounds of fighting echoed all around. As the

group dashed out into the center of the stage toward the ghost light stand, Ridley managed to grab a microphone from the proscenium, dragging the cord behind her.

"This way," said the Other Mr. Vernon, turning toward the stage doors. But that direction was blocked by several of the mesmerized townspeople, who were chanting. *"What have I done? What have I done?"*

There was no way out—not from up here, not unless they were willing to plow through these people, risking injury or worse.

Ridley thought again about the note she had not left for her mother, and a coolness came upon her skin. Maybe it was the evening air wafting in from outside, or maybe it was something else, something that was inside her. The people blocking the way to the loading dock and the people fighting in the orchestra seats were her neighbors and acquaintances. They were the people her mom sped past on the street, the people who made Mineral Wells what it was. If Ridley didn't do something, if she plowed right past everyone to the exit, she'd become exactly like her mother. She had to stop all of this.

And she had an idea of how.

She flipped the power switch on the cord, and the speakers at the front of the stage came alive. She tapped the mic, and the sound resonated around the room. For a moment, it seemed as though everyone might suddenly halt what they were doing, but the moment passed and the fighting continued.

"Friends!" Ridley called out. "Please!" The room hushed and all the faces turned toward her. "Stop what you're doing. I beg you. We know the truth. A horrible man has been recording you for months. He knows all your secrets, your deepest embarrassments, and your worst fears. He'll reveal everything if you don't do his bidding. But this is not worth whatever secret you think you need to keep!"

An electric buzzing filled the room as the single bulb on the ghost light stand began to dim. It flickered briefly and then went out.

Chaos erupted again—the sounds of scuffling in the darkness.

There came a loud *click*, and the stage suddenly flooded with light. Ridley blinked and held up her hand, shading her eyes. To her horror, she noticed that several townspeople had slipped into the slim space between the guardians and the Misfits.

Ridley and her friends had been corralled next to the steep drop-off by the orchestra pit. The mesmerized people on the stage with them were holding garden tools from the caretaker's shed as weapons. Pitchforks, shears, rusted shovels caked with hard earth. They pointed them at the guardians and at the Vernons, who stood helpless with their hands raised.

Magic tricks would be no defense now.

There was a ripple of shadow in the corner of Ridley's vision, and when she turned, she saw a man standing next to the ghost light. His top hat was tilted mockingly, and his black cloak draped down to the floor. His collar still hid his face, but everyone here knew who he was. The fighting instantly stopped as all of the mesmerized townspeople turned to face their tormentor and master. Kalagan chuckled, then undid the bow under his chin. The cloak dropped to the floor as he knocked the hat away, revealing an ordinary-looking man dressed in denim jeans and a wrinkled beige linen shirt. Ridley knew that face. She'd seen it earlier in the week, in the alleyway behind the abandoned movie theater.

It really was Carter's uncle Sly.

It was Kalagan.

They were one and the same.

He tilted his face toward the light, like someone who was seeing the sun for the first time in decades, and then raised his hands to the crowd. "Welcome, everyone, at long last, to our grand finale!" Ridley expected the mesmerized people to break into applause, but only confused silence followed. Her friends huddled close to her chair. Ridley had never felt so helpless. Kalagan dipped his head as if bowing. "I have asked you here this evening to celebrate Mineral Wells's *golden son*." He held out his hand to Mr. Vernon. "Come on, Dante. Take a bow!"

One of Kalagan's cronies moved toward the Vernons with a shovel, forcing them apart. Dante stepped away from his husband and the guardians and into Kalagan's spotlight. He did not bow. Instead, he looked to the Misfits, tears welling in his eyes. This frightened Ridley more than anything that had come before. If Mr. Vernon had lost hope, what did that mean for the rest of them?

"I said bow," Kalagan growled.

Mr. Vernon only glared at the man. "What do you want, Kilroy?" he asked.

"Oh-ho," Kalagan chortled. "What a question. Why

don't you ask the children?" He glanced to the Misfits. "They've been doing their research. Apparently, they know all about what I want and what I need."

"I'm asking you," Mr. Vernon insisted with an air of calm.

This seemed to annoy the man. He grumbled to himself for a moment before regaining his composure and directing his voice to the auditorium once more. "What I *want*, Dante, is to get what's coming to me. What I *deserve*. And I want the members of your Magic Circle to see you for what you are. A weak-minded, treacherous, sniveling villain, who lied, cheated, and manipulated his way to where he is today."

"Have you looked in the mirror lately, Kilroy?" Mr. Vernon answered. "Because it sounds to me like you're talking about yourself."

"Your Magic Circle *will* join me," Kalagan spat out. "I have ways of making people do what I want them to do."

"*Obviously*," Mr. Vernon said, rolling his eyes. He sounded a bit like Leila when she was being cheeky. Ridley understood what he was doing. Mr. Vernon was trying to distract Kalagan, to keep his attention off the Misfits and his children.

(I'll say it again: *Classic misdirection!*)

A large man wearing a tight suit and a thin woman dressed in a red dress and strings of pearls stood before the Misfits, blocking their way. Ridley wondered if her chair would survive a tumble off the edge of the stage and down to the orchestra pit. *No chance*, she thought grimly.

"We've wasted enough time!" Kalagan called out. "You *will* have your Circle give me their names, Dante. And as a thank-you for running me around these past few months, I will allow *you* to perform the last act of this grand finale, as you were so desperate to do back when we were kids, on the night you set this very building on fire."

A murmuring rose up from the people in the audience, and more scuffling broke out as the townspeople held back members of Vernon's Magic Circle. Ridley heard a shriek and an *oof!*, then more silence. Kalagan waved forward several of his people standing at the back of the stage. They wheeled in a large object from just outside. The wheels squealed as the townspeople moved the object into the spotlight. Ridley's ears began to ring when she realized what it was: the wreckage of her invention.

Her magic box.

She heard her friends gasp as they saw it too. Mr. Vernon kept his face blank as he watched the towns-people stand the box on end. It was not the first time that Ridley realized it looked like a coffin.

It was banged up, covered in scratches, but Kalagan or his people had done some quick work since retriev-ing it from the lake a couple of hours earlier. Some-one had replaced the lid that Ridley had dropped at the mouth of the cave, as well as the side panels that Olly and Izzy had used as oars to steer them to shore. There were also several metal loops attached to the sides of the box—something Ridley had not added herself.

Kalagan crossed to the magic box and swung the lid open. The squeak of the hinges made Ridley think of Dean and about what they had done to him.

Locking him in there.

Her skin itched with guilt.

Where was Dean now? Ridley wondered, glancing around the room. But the old man was nowhere to be seen. Was it possible that the bellhop was hiding in the shadows, waiting to save the day? Maybe he'd decided that whatever Kalagan was holding over him was not worth all this hurt.

Ridley felt another shift in her head, as a new

thought occurred to her. She gripped the microphone tightly.

"Get in," Kalagan said, grabbing Mr. Vernon's arm, but Mr. Vernon shook him off. More sounds of fighting came from the dark auditorium. Ridley was cheered to think that the members of the Circle were still trying to get to them, even if they were horribly outnumbered.

"Don't touch him!" the Other Mr. Vernon yelled from the darkness upstage.

"I'm fine, darling," Mr. Vernon called back. "He has no power over me."

"That's what *you* think," said Kalagan, flicking his gaze to the man in the suit and the woman in the pearls who were corralling the Misfits at the edge of the stage. "But I know your weakness, Dante. I've watched for years now. I know what matters to you." He nodded at Leila and at Carter. "Your family. You'd do anything for them."

"Leave the kids alone," Mr. Vernon said, his voice quiet, simmering intensely.

"I intend to," Kalagan answered. "If you follow my instructions." He opened the lid of the magic box even wider. "Get in," he repeated. "I won't ask a third time."

"Don't listen to him, Dad!" Leila shouted.

Mr. Vernon hesitated. "Don't worry," Kalagan said, almost jovially. "I'll give you time to escape. I'm not a *monster*. If you can make it out before it's too late, you win. I'll let you and your family go. And all these fine people"—he waved at the mesmerized audience—"they can get back to their ordinary lives."

"No, Dante! Don't trust him!" Carter yelled.

Mr. Vernon gazed at the Misfits for a long moment, then sighed. "I love you all," he said before stepping inside the magic box. Kalagan slammed the lid shut and began to laugh.

TWENTY-FOUR

As if from nowhere, a length of chain appeared in Kalagan's hands. Within seconds, he'd managed to wind it through the new metal loops that were attached to the sides of the box. In the center of the lid, right over the spot where Ridley imagined Mr. Vernon's heart was hidden inside, Kalagan attached a thick brass lock. He waved his people forward. In their arms, they carried thin pieces of kindling and several chunks of firewood, which they arranged at the base of the box as they whisper-chanted, *"What have I done? What have I done?"*

"Let him go!" Leila shrieked. She tried to rush forward, but one of the lackeys pushed her roughly back.

Kalagan brought his mouth close to the box. "I will give you the same chance of escape that you gave to my parents that night, years ago," he said. "The night they perished in a fire that *you* set." He glanced at Leila and the rest of the Misfits. "Don't worry, children. If he's as good a magician as he believes he is, Dante Vernon will be free in no time!" He snapped his fingers and a flame appeared in his palm. Kalagan bent and held the fire to the kindling. It caught quickly, white smoke seeping out, spreading into the spotlight that shone from above.

Ridley had full faith that Mr. Vernon was as good a magician as any magician who ever magicianed. But the odds were stacked against him. There was no way Kalagan didn't have this whole thing rigged so Mr. Vernon would fail. She looked out over the auditorium seats, where many of the townspeople still stood holding the members of Mr. Vernon's Magic Circle at bay. She could see several of them grappling, trying to reach the stage, but there were simply too many opponents. The Circle was overwhelmed. She held the microphone up. "You're good people," she said. "I know you are. We're neighbors. I see what's important to you. We cannot let this happen."

"What are you doing, Ridley?" Theo whispered in her ear.

"Would someone shut her up?" Kalagan called out to the townspeople. Some of the men who'd brought over the firewood ran offstage, following the microphone cord.

Ridley could hear Mr. Vernon moving around inside the magic box. The smell of smoke was growing stronger. They were running out of time!

"This man has no power over you!" Ridley waved her hand at Kalagan, who stared back at her, his eyes filled with the memory of fire. "He's no mesmerist. No hypnotist. No all-powerful sorcerer. He is a sad man who has manipulated you. But you can stop him! You can share your secret. Speak it out loud. Break the spell!"

To her surprise, she found that the audience was listening to her.

"*I* have a secret," she went on. "Something that worries me day and night. I thought I would die if I ever told anyone. But I won't die. And neither will you.

I'm willing to tell my secret in order to destroy Kala-gan's power. The question is: Are you willing too?"

Murmuring spread slowly through the auditorium.

"My secret is that..." Ridley took a deep breath, then said, "I'm-afraid-my-mother-doesn't-love-me-as-much-as-she-loves-her-work." The words flew out of Ridley's mouth like sparks. No way to retrieve them now. "And I'm afraid that I'm too much like her, that I steamroll people and make them feel unwanted. I'm afraid—"

The microphone cut out. Ridley wasn't sure she could have gone on anyway. She felt warm arms embrace her from behind. Turning her head, she saw Theo's face.

"I have a secret too," he shouted out, his voice surprisingly strong. "Over the summer...I lost one of my pet doves. She just flew off. I worry that it was because I neglected her in some way. I feel so irresponsible. I never told anyone. I think about her all the time and dream that she is soaring into a never-ending sunset."

Ridley grabbed Theo's forearm and squeezed. She looked over her shoulder at the magic box. The kindling was glowing brighter. Small flames had crept up onto the firewood. She examined the faces of the nearest townspeople, but their eyes were still hardened and glassy.

"My secret is..." Carter began with a deep gulp. "I always tell people that I *never steal*..." He let out a shiver. "But when I lived with my uncle Sly..." He kept his eyes averted from the man standing near the box. "I went to bed hungry all the time. So...sometimes, when we passed a market, I would pocket a piece of fruit to save for later, in case there was no next meal." Ridley took Carter's hand, and he glanced down at her with a sad smile.

"That's enough," Kalagan shouted.

"*My* secret?" Leila yelled, as if she just wanted to get this out of the way. "I helped someone very close to me get away from the police."

"Shut their mouths!"

But the townspeople continued to listen.

Olly went next. "I worry that I'm not actually very funny at all," he said.

Izzy raised her hand sheepishly. "I *also* worry that my brother is not very funny," she said.

A few people in the crowd chuckled, including the man in the suit and the woman in pearls who were still holding the Misfits at the edge of the stage. Ridley looked to the man. "And you, sir? Are you willing to share what you don't want people to know?" The man glared at her for a moment before releasing a deep breath. He checked the magic box. The firewood was on the verge of becoming engulfed. Once that happened, Ridley knew it would be minutes until the flames ate up her contraption—along with Dante Vernon.

"You'll be sorry," Kalagan warned the man.

"No, I won't," the man spat back. "This is reprehensible....My secret is that I owe a large gambling debt!" he shouted to the room. "And I never told my family. I'm so, so sorry. I plan on paying it all back. It's just that...it's gotten out of control."

The audience conferred with one another. Their murmuring grew louder.

Kalagan glared out at them. He stepped to the front of the stage. "I've got the tapes. I'll spread your secrets far and wide. Your lives will *never* be the same."

Silence descended. In the quiet, the crackling of the fire echoed through the auditorium. The magic box shuddered as Mr. Vernon pounded from the inside, the chains rattling like grim bells.

Ridley couldn't take anymore. "Please!" she yelled. She didn't know what else to say. Her throat felt red and raw.

Leila screamed, tears staining her face. "You're killing him!" She fell to her knees. Carter dropped down and threw his arms around her.

Whispers came from the first few rows of seats. "How can we allow this?"

"It isn't right."

"Vernon's not escaping!"

"We've got to help him!"

A voice called out from the audience. Another secret. "I hit a car in the church parking lot and then drove away!"

And another. "I lied to my mom about my grades!"

And another. "I dropped my baby brother when we were young. He cracked his skull. I never told my parents."

More voices rose up, overlapping.

"I have another family in another town!"

"I stole money from my boss!"

"I'm in love with my neighbor!"

"I'm not who I say I am!"

Ridley was shocked by these secrets.

But she knew they didn't matter anymore. What mattered was that the spell was breaking.

The fire grew stronger. Orange embers fell away from the firewood and landed on the stage.

"Listen to me!" Kalagan shrieked. "I will destroy you! I will destroy everything!"

Panicked voices rose up over the others. "Let Vernon out!" the people called.

"Grab the fire extinguisher!"

"Call the fire department!"

Wide-eyed, the man in the suit and the woman in the pearls finally stepped aside. The Misfits rushed toward the burning box.

The guardians broke away from the people with the garden tools. They darted toward Kalagan.

At the front of the stage, Kalagan whirled at the sudden chaos. For the first time, he looked frightened. He knew he was losing. He glanced down into the orchestra pit and considered a leap. His pause was just long enough for Sandra Santos to tackle him to the floor. The other guardians held him down as he thrashed and screamed.

The base of the magic box was smoking, about to ignite.

Ridley shouted, "Help!"

The Other Mr. Vernon snatched away the garden tools from the dazed townspeople. He tossed a shovel to Carter and a pickaxe to Leila, both of whom used the blades to sweep the burning wood away from the bottom of the box. The embers scattered, and Carter and Leila dashed about, trying to stomp them out.

Ridley moved beside the still-smoking box. "Olly!

Izzy! We've got to knock this over. Give me a hand!"
She directed the twins to shove at the top half of the
box as she kept the bottom in place with her footrests.
They weren't strong enough, but then the Other Mr.
Vernon bounded over. As the box began to tilt, Ridley
swiveled her chair out of the way.

"Hold tight, Mr. Vernon!" she called out as the box
tipped and crashed to the blackened stage. The chains
were still wrapped tightly around the lid, the brass lock
looking too complicated for even Leila to crack. Instead,
Ridley flipped up a soot-covered latch from the bottom panel, nearly burning the tips of her fingers. The
floor of the box fell down to the scorched stage floor,
revealing a pair of feet. A voice groaned from inside.
The Other Mr. Vernon knelt down and grabbed at his
husband's calves.

A moment later, the Other Mr. Vernon cradled
Dante in his arms. The magician's suit was still smoking. He began coughing violently, then let out a low
groan. "Well, well," he said weakly, then coughed
again. "That was a hot one."

★ ★ ★

By the time the ambulances and fire trucks arrived, most of the townspeople had scattered into the night.

Many members of Vernon's Magic Circle hid around the Grand Oak theater as the police took Kilroy Kalagan away in handcuffs. The guardians watched from the stage wings, as if this had all been a play and they were waiting to take a final bow.

After it was done, Ridley and the other Misfits rode with Quinn the concierge to the hospital where the ambulance had taken the Vernons. The doctors told the group that he was suffering from smoke inhalation. He also had some minor burns.

"I'm so sorry, Mr. Vernon," Ridley said at Dante's bedside. His nose and mustache were covered by an oxygen mask. "I wish I could have broken Kalagan's spell faster."

"You were incredible," said the Other Mr. Vernon. "We wouldn't be here now if it weren't for your quick thinking. All of you."

The Misfits gathered around the bed. Mr. Vernon reached up to remove his oxygen mask. "Only for a moment, darling," he assured the Other Mr. Vernon. "I must tell these children how sorry I am—no, Ridley,

I *must* apologize for the secrets that I never should have kept, and then we will leave it to rest for good. I am so thankful to have each and every one of you in my life, and I promise never again to be anything less than honest, as you all were so bravely tonight, sharing your secrets and fears."

Mr. Vernon returned his mask to his nose and mouth and took a few slow, deep breaths. The Other Mr. Vernon looked worried, but smiled as his husband removed the mask again to continue.

"Carter: You've been through more than any young person should, and not one of us would begrudge you an extra mouthful of food. The help you've given others outweighs tenfold a necessary past thievery." Carter ducked his head, though Ridley saw a smile on his face.

"Leila: My wonderful girl, nor would any of us judge you your past decisions, made in an effort to help someone as well. You are so good and so kind, and I know you always will be." Leila's face was covered in tears as she reached out to hold her father's hand.

"Theo: So thoughtful and considerate. We could no more think that you neglected your doves than believe a word out of Kalagan's mouth. Let us instead remember your bird fondly, knowing it is soaring through the sky on its own adventure.

"And Ridley: You saved us all with your quick thinking and willingness to admit a great secret. I know I cannot reassure you of your mother's love, though I am certain it is far stronger than you know. But I can make sure you realize how beloved you are by everyone in this room." Releasing his fingers from Leila, he took Ridley's hand and squeezed it tightly.

Ridley was so taken aback by this declaration that she could only nod and rub a tear off her cheek. In fact, both Vernons and all Misfits were sniffling and smiling, looking to one another in happiness and relief that all was forgiven, and that they were finally safe.

(I've gone through an entire box of tissues myself since the start of this scene!)

"Hey, what about us?" Olly said.

"Yeah, what about the secrets we revealed?" Izzy echoed.

Mr. Vernon took another breath from his mask, then began coughing violently. Leila rubbed his hand as the Other Mr. Vernon rang for a nurse.

"We're sorry, Mr. Vernon!" said Olly.

"Never mind!" Izzy added.

"No, no," Mr. Vernon replied between coughs. "It is only—ha—only that—"

"Stop trying to speak, for goodness' sake, Dante," the Other Mr. Vernon chided.

Bent almost double, Mr. Vernon let out a sudden "Ha! Haha! I'm sorry, everyone. It's only that the thought of Olly and Izzy *not* being funny is the silliest thing I've ever heard. No one has ever made me laugh as hard as the two of you."

Izzy and Olly beamed.

"Thanks a lot, Mr. Vernon," Ridley said, though she was grinning too. "There'll be no stopping their shenanigans now."

⋆ ⋆ ⋆

When Ridley left the room to call her mother, she noticed a black mark on her palm. Looking closer, she saw that it was Mr. Vernon's symbol—the ace of spades. She wanted to laugh and cry at the same time. Even in his sorry condition, Mr. Vernon was still trying to make magic.

(Haven't I told you from the beginning that the world will always need more magic?)

Mrs. Larsen answered the phone after the first ring. "Ridley?" She sounded upset.

"Hi, Mom," she said, trying to tamp down the quaver in her throat.

"Where are you?"

"There was...an incident. At the hotel. Everything is fine, but Mr. Vernon is at the hospital. My friends and I are staying with him for a while."

Without hesitation, Mrs. Larsen answered, "All right. I'm on my way."

"Thanks, Mom. I'll see you soon."

Ridley hung up the phone and was halfway back to Mr. Vernon's room before realizing her mother hadn't rambled even once.

HOW TO...

Guess a Card in the Middle of the Deck

After being put through the emotional ringer, I bet you're ready for another magic lesson. I know I am! And this is a favorite of mine, because once you practice it to perfection, you can use it as the base for many other tricks to impress your friends, family, and random passersby. Just like any sport or other skill, when you master a basic move, you're well on your way to mastering even bigger and better ones. Now enough jabbering—let's learn how to guess an audience member's card from the middle of the deck.

WHAT YOU'LL NEED:

- A deck of cards
- A roll of tape
- A volunteer

TO PREPARE:

1. For this trick, you'll need to create a double-backed card. Simply take two cards from the deck and tape them together so that the backs of the cards are both facing outward.

2. Memorize the card on the top of the deck. (For example, let's say it's the king of hearts.)

3. Turn the top card over so that it alone is facing up.

4. Place the double-backed card on top of the top card.

STEPS:

1. Explain to your volunteer that you will attempt to guess their card.

2. Briefly show the deck to the volunteer, then use your thumb to riffle through the cards.

3. Ask them to tell you when to stop riffling. Point to the card you've stopped on and tell the volunteer that this is the card they've picked.

4. Separate the deck into two piles. Point out that the card they've "picked" is on top of the second pile.

5. Turn the first pile over and place it on top of the second pile, explaining that this is how you're "marking" their card.

SECRET MAGIC MOVE

Turning the first pile over will invert the first two
cards of the deck, the double-backer and the card
you've memorized—in this case, the king of hearts.
All the cards in the first pile will now be facing up,
except for the two inverted cards.

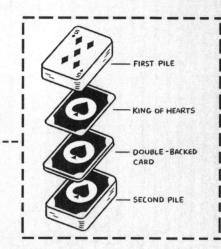

FIRST PILE

KING OF HEARTS

DOUBLE-BACKED
CARD

SECOND PILE

6. Shuffle through the faceup cards until you get to the first facedown card. Your volunteer will think that *this* is the card they stopped on.

7. Concentrate on "guessing" the card (really play it up!) and then tell your volunteer that you're sure they've chosen the king of hearts, or whichever card you've forced them to choose.

8. Turn the card over. *Wow* them!

9. Take a well-deserved bow!

— TWENTY-FIVE —

A couple of days later, Leila and Carter invited Ridley to see the spot where the Vernons were considering rebuilding the magic shop. This was news to Ridley, so she begged Ms. Parkly to take her after their lessons were finished.

A taxi brought them up the road into the hills past the Grand Oak Resort. The car let them off at the foot of a long driveway that stretched up a slope where a sprawling house sat. It was made of turrets and porches and porticos and cupolas and wooden curlicue decorations.

(Don't you just love vocabulary? When you say architecture words aloud—*portico! cupola! curlicue!*—it almost sounds like a magic spell, doesn't it?)

Ridley had never owned a dollhouse, but if she had, she imagined it would have looked something like this. The drive was overgrown with weeds and brush and a thin layer of colorful fallen leaves. As Ridley and Ms. Parkly made their way up the hill, they could see that the mansion was in similar disrepair. Like so many beautiful old houses, it needed help.

Several cars were parked in the turnabout. Out front, Ridley recognized the Other Mr. Vernon's station wagon, but she didn't know who the others belonged to.

Ridley rolled up the front ramp and knocked on the door, Ms. Parkly just behind her.

A moment later, Leila and Carter greeted her with enormous grins. "Come in!" said Carter.

"Isn't this *fabulous*?" asked Leila, leading the way into a grand foyer with creaky wood floors and a falling down ceiling. "It used to belong to my dad's aunt. She left it to him a few years ago, but he and Poppa said they didn't have any use for it."

"We finally convinced them that it would be the perfect spot for a new version of the magic shop," said Carter. "And the kitchen is big enough for the Other Mr. Vernon to try out a heap of new recipes. Who cares that it's not in the center of the village? After *we're* done with it, everyone will go out of their way to come visit."

"I know I will," said Ridley.

"So much potential!" said Ms. Parkly.

"Everyone is waiting in the sitting room," said Leila, waving them forward.

"Who's *everyone*?" Ridley asked.

Carter slid open a pair of double doors. Inside, a group of people sitting in folding chairs turned to look at them. Both Vernons, Theo, the Golden twins, and the guardians—Gregor, Tara, Quinn, Peter the pet store clerk, and Sandra Santos, whose bright, star-shaped earrings dangled from her ears, as always.

"Ridley!" said Mr. Vernon, struggling to stand, but the Other Mr. Vernon made him sit down again. A thin green canister was set up on wheels beside him, a clear tube leading from it into Mr. Vernon's nostrils. He saw Ridley flinch at the sight and held up his hand to explain. "It's oxygen. My doctor says I'll need it for the next few days. Nothing to worry about." He rubbed his fingers together and another clear tube appeared in his hand. "Want some?" Everyone laughed.

"He has done the same trick to each of us," said Theo, who stood and led Ridley to a bright spot near the portico windows.

"What can I say?" Mr. Vernon responded. "I guess I'm already feeling better."

"I think we all are," Ridley answered.

"How wonderful to hear!" said Mr. Vernon.

"Does this mean that the Magic Misfits are allowed to meet again?" Carter asked.

"It's well past time," said Mr. Vernon. "I can't apologize enough that my actions have kept you from practicing your magic."

"We've been practicing, Dad," said Leila. "Don't you worry."

"I wish I had something delicious to offer you all," said the Other Mr. Vernon. "But this place doesn't even have running water yet."

The group spent some time chatting and catching up. The guardians told bits and pieces of their own stories of how they'd come to find Mr. Vernon's Magic Circle. Sandra Santos apologized to the Misfits once more.

"I have a question," said Theo. "In the Grand Oak theater, Leila said she helped someone escape from the police. Was that you, Sandra?"

Sandra smiled. "That's not my secret to reveal."

Everyone looked to Leila, who turned pink and then shrugged. "I've said all I'm going to say. Some secrets are worth keeping."

They told tales of what they'd heard had happened to the mesmerized citizens over the past couple of days, and how things around town were already seeming like normal. Ridley had a hard time believing that, but she knew it wouldn't be worth arguing at the moment. Maybe later, but now was a time for reunion.

Leila and Carter had just offered to give everyone a tour when there was a knock at the door.

"Who else knows we're here?" Mr. Vernon whispered to the Other Mr. Vernon.

The Other Mr. Vernon shook his head, then went to check. A moment later, Ridley heard shouting in the entryway. "Get out!" the Other Mr. Vernon yelled. "We don't want what you're selling."

Ridley followed the others down the hall to find a stooped man standing in the doorway—Dean the bellhop.

"It's all right," Mr. Vernon said from the shadows as he wheeled his oxygen tank along beside himself. "Let the man in."

Ridley crossed her arms. Was this a good idea? Dean had betrayed them, after all.

Dean stepped across the threshold before anyone could stop him. He closed the door. "Thank you, Mr. V.," he said through chattering teeth. His bellhop uniform was dirty and ragged, as if he'd been camping in the woods without a tent. Or maybe in the mouth of a cave. "I'm sorry to bother you all. But I've got something to say. I was hoping you might be willing to listen and maybe lend a hand with a problem I'm having."

The Other Mr. Vernon stood beside his husband, wrapping an arm around his waist and propping him up. "Always willing to listen, Dean," said Mr. Vernon.

Dean nodded. "Much appreciated." He removed his hat and smoothed his hand over his scalp. Somehow, it seemed as though his thin hair was suddenly thick. Darker. He removed a handkerchief from his jacket pocket and dabbed at his forehead.

Something didn't feel right to Ridley.

Moving his gaze to meet each of the Misfits' eyes, Dean went on. "You're all aware that I was assisting the man you know as Kalagan."

"We remember," said Ridley, feeling a hardness stuck in her voice.

Dean's eyes fell on her. "I told you some things about him back when we were all in the cave together. But like most stories"—he paused—"the one I told you was only part of the truth. To get to the other part, I'll need to take you back in time."

Ridley glanced at her friends scattered around the entry foyer. All of them looked as confused—and maybe a little nervous—as she felt. She was glad their guardians were with them.

"Several decades, in fact," Dean went on. "To a time before the Emerald Ring had even been imagined."

Mr. Vernon flinched, concern passing across his face like a cloud. "I'm sorry, Dean, but what's this about? Kalagan is in jail."

"I'm getting to that, Mr. V.," Dean answered. "Now, all of you know I've been working at the Grand Oak for a long time. The story I need to share has to do with a couple other employees of the resort—a husband and wife pair of housekeepers named Augustus and Diana Kalagan."

"Kilroy's parents," Theo whispered.

"That's right." Dean nodded, dabbing his face with the handkerchief again. As he did so, his skin seemed to brighten, the gray circles under his eyes beginning to fade. "Augustus and Diana lived here in Mineral Wells. And they had quite a few secrets of their own. Though they were honorable employees of our town's fabled resort, they made money in other ways. Ways in which Carter is probably familiar."

"Wait," said Carter, growing pale. "What?"

But Dean went on. "They were grifters. Con artists.

They had run the shell game up and down the coast for years before finding stability in Mineral Wells. But they were always dreaming bigger. Augustus especially. When his wife gave birth to twin boys—Kilroy and Kincaid—he hatched a scheme for what he hoped might turn into his biggest con ever. A con for the record books." Dean cleared his throat...and slowly began to straighten his spine.

Was he suddenly taller? Ridley wondered, nervous energy coursing through her. *How could that be?*

"It took some convincing to get his wife to agree, but Augustus managed to make it look like one of the twin boys had died. He and Diana buried a tiny casket in the local cemetery. Even got the kid a grave marker that said his age had been less than a year. The truth was much more sinister." The room was silent, except for the mice scurrying through the walls. "You see, Augustus believed that if he could make the world think that they had only one son, he and his wife could get away with so much more. Often, one twin would outright steal from hotel employees, while Augustus made sure someone witnessed the other twin being perfectly innocent during the time of the theft, so that no one could accuse him of the crime.

"One of the family's favorite tricks was to have one twin disappear around a corner as the other would come up behind a hotel guest and shout *hello*. Startled, the guest always thought they'd witnessed some sort of impossible teleportation. As the guest tried to figure out how Kilroy had done it, they were too distracted to notice when Kincaid came back and picked their pockets."

Ridley felt like she couldn't breathe. But she could not stop listening to Dean's tale. Everyone else seemed just as transfixed, especially as Dean was now standing perfectly straight, a feat none of them had thought possible for the old man.

"Kilroy and Kincaid. The Kalagan boys. Or *boy*, as they had everyone believing. Augustus and Diana taught their sons everything they knew. And when the brothers made friends in town with a ragtag group of kid magicians, they began to learn even more tricks. They grew preoccupied with the idea of mesmerism. Because the thing was, being raised as one person made the twins feel like they had no control over their lives. Manipulating *other* people felt to them like real magic. And life with their new friends felt like real magic too."

Ridley glanced at Mr. Vernon, who looked utterly baffled. Dean gave one last swipe of the handkerchief across his mouth. He held up the cloth, presenting it to the group as if it were part of a magic trick. And Ridley supposed that it was; the handkerchief was smudged with what looked like makeup.

"The magic died on the day of the West Lodge fire." Now Dean started scratching at the base of his nose, his eyes continuously moving from one Misfit to the next, then to the Vernons, and back to each Misfit, as if he wanted to be sure they couldn't look away. "With their parents gone, Kilroy and Kincaid decided to keep up the charade. But living at Mother Margaret's Home was difficult, especially since only one of them could show their face at any given moment. The other had to stay out on the streets, hot or cold, rain or shine, sleet or snow. They switched places every night so that each could be fed and sleep in a bed and wash up. And that's how they spent the next few years. Lying. Faking. Cheating. Just getting by. They always remembered what their parents taught them, and they made it work, better than Augustus and Diana ever could."

To Ridley's horror, Dean suddenly pulled what

looked like a flap of skin right off his face—and his whole nose with it! *Ugh!* But there was something underneath... *It's a prosthetic*, she realized. *A fake nose, on a fake face, on a body made to look much older than it really was.*

Throwing the pretend nose to the ground, Dean quickly unbuttoned his jacket and slipped that off too. Underneath was a white tank top. When he ran his hands through his hair once more, he looked like a totally different person.

He looked like Carter's uncle Sly.

He looked like *Kalagan.*

Ridley nearly screamed. Carter and Leila grabbed at each other's hands. Olly and Izzy hopped, skipped, and jumped to their guardians' sides as Theo's face paled and his eyes grew huge. Ridley felt Ms. Parkly's hand suddenly on her shoulder. The Other Mr. Vernon struggled to hold up his husband, who had sagged at the revelation.

Dean the bellhop had not only been a disguise. He had been an act—a performance to rival those at the

Grand Oak theater. *This had to be a dream,* Ridley thought. A nightmare.

Dean's eyes darted to Carter, whose mouth was a perfect O. "Hello, boy," he said, his voice suddenly raspy. Carter stumbled backward, nearly hitting the wall. "Recognize me? You wondered how your uncle Sly could be in so many places at once? Same thing with our Kalagan character. It was a cinch when there were *two* of us."

"Kincaid?" Mr. Vernon asked gently, as if speaking any louder might set off a box of TNT.

The man who had been Dean nodded. "Yes, Dante?"

"You stated at the beginning that you want us to lend you a hand. What kind of hand would that be?"

"I want you to get Kilroy out of the Mineral Wells Jail."

"You know we can't do that," the Other Mr. Vernon said warily.

"I know you *can*. Leila gave her skeleton key to Sandra Santos over the summer." His dark eyes flipped to Sandra's face. "You must still have it."

"I—I don't," Sandra stammered. "Not here. Not anymore."

Ridley couldn't tell if the woman was lying—it had once been her job after all.

Dean stepped forward.

Or Kincaid, rather.

No...

Kalagan.

Let's just call him Kalagan.

Kalagan stepped forward, placing his hands into his pants pockets. Did he have a weapon? Ridley was too far away from him to fight him with her chair. "You're going to get my brother out of there," Kalagan demanded. "We've never been apart this long before. I...I don't know what to do without him."

"What do you need us for? You'll figure it out," said Mr. Vernon. "You're a crafty man, Kincaid."

"No, *you'll* figure it out," Kalagan said, his voice growing louder. "You always figure out *everything*. All of you. You'll use your magic skills to distract the officers. You'll sneak the key down the hallway to the cell. You'll—"

Carter stomped his foot, his cheeks flushing red. "If you think we're going to help you and your lunatic twin..."

Kalagan whipped his head around and growled

at Carter. "If you don't help me out, I will *never* stop coming for you."

When he paused, Ridley saw something in his gaze that she thought she might be able to use. But did she dare? Was she going to try to manipulate a *master manipulator*? And did that make her just as bad as him?

"You weren't there," she said quickly. "Were you?"

He raised an eyebrow. "What are you talking about?"

"Onstage. In the auditorium. That was Kilroy."

"So what?"

"They were *his* plans. Not yours. You never would have gone as far as *he* tried to."

Kalagan opened his mouth to retort, but nothing came out.

"You don't want to hurt us," Ridley said. "You never did. I can see it in your eyes. That was *Kilroy*." She looked to the others. They nodded.

Leila chimed in. "You loved your brother so much that you went along with what he said. Isn't that right?"

Kalagan's silence spoke volumes.

"You can *still* be together," Ridley said slowly.

"But you won't help me." Kalagan's voice sounded childlike and elderly at the same time.

"I *will* help you," said Ridley.

"We all will," Theo offered.

"We can head down to the station together," Ridley went on. "But instead of breaking Kilroy out, you'll turn yourself in."

"What? No!" Kalagan scoffed.

"Yes," said Ridley. "I can't even imagine how difficult your life has been. Living this lie. This trick."

"Always having to be separate from Kilroy," said Olly. "Never being seen together."

"You told us your secret, Kincaid," Theo added. "You broke the spell. It is over."

Carter sniffed and then wiped at his nose. "You don't need to *lie* anymore."

"You can be with your best friend," said Izzy, grabbing Olly's hand. "Your brother."

"People change," said Leila, glancing at her fathers. "My dad changed when he sent you that apology letter when you were kids."

"Kilroy ripped it up," Kalagan replied. "I was the one who kept the pieces."

"And you're changing now," Ridley went on. "Transforming. Right before our eyes." Everyone was quiet for a moment. Kalagan stared at the floor. Was it possible that he was really listening? Taking it in? "Someone," Ridley said, looking at Ms. Parkly, "once told the Magic Misfits that *together we are strong*." The teacher nodded, her strawberry-blond bob bouncing. "You and your brother were taught that strength comes from power."

"From control," said Theo.

"And manipulation," said Carter.

"From the things you could steal," said Izzy.

"From what you thought you owned," Olly added.

"Those things aren't real," said Leila. "They're illusions."

"I believe that what makes all of us strong is family. Togetherness." Ridley looked at the group. The Other Mr. Vernon was still holding up his husband. Leila and Carter stood side by side. Theo rested his hand on Ridley's shoulder. Olly and Izzy clasped hands. Ridley thought of her mother typing diligently at home and of her father working on the road. She imagined a time when they could all be together again.

"Honesty is strength," said Ms. Parkly.

"And forgiveness," said Sandra.

"They're right," Mr. Vernon told his old nemesis.

"These are the things that make us stronger. Stronger on the *inside*."

(Which, if I do say so myself, is the strongest type of strength that exists.)

The rest of the guardians stepped toward Kalagan, forming a circle around him. Ridley slowly reached into the panel in her chair that usually held pencil and paper, but now held Leila's thumb-cuffs, which she'd forgotten at Ridley's house a few days ago. "I'm sure you have all sorts of tricks up your sleeve to fight us now," she said. "And knowing you, you'll probably get in a few good jabs before we take you down again."

"But that is not what you are here for, is it?" asked Theo.

"You didn't *really* come to fight," said Leila.

"The fight is over," Carter finished.

Ridley gestured to each person standing beside her in that grand and crumbling foyer. "These are my friends. My family. They have helped me so much over the past few years. And especially over the past few months. I've changed because I've let them in. I let them see me. All the good and all the bad that exists inside me. Together we are strong. You can change too. You *and* your brother."

Kalagan hung his head. Was his lip quivering? Was this *actually* working?

Ridley moved to his side. She gently clicked the cuffs around his thumbs. "Others can only help you along so much," she said. "You have to do the rest yourself."

—TWENTY-SIX—

You can probably guess what happened next.

No! Kalagan did not attack everybody and then blow up the Vernons' new house!

He listened to the Magic Misfits. He took Ridley's advice.

Before the end of that day, Kincaid Kalagan was sitting in the cell in the police station in the center of Mineral Wells, next to his twin brother.

They were together. At last.

And boy was Kilroy angry!

People said later, you could hear them fighting

from down the street, but that was only until they were moved to the bigger jail in Bell's Landing.

After that, no one heard from them for many years.

* * *

By the end of the week, most of the guardians had left Mineral Wells, easing their way back into the lives they had left to come and help Dante Vernon. The Magic Misfits were on their own again.

Mrs. Larsen was troubled by Ms. Parkly's abrupt departure, but rather than hiring a new teacher, she abruptly declared that she'd decided to take back the homeschooling responsibility now that her deadline was over. Over the next few weeks, Ridley sometimes missed Ms. Parkly's discussions and the way she'd tried so hard and how clumsy she'd pretended to be—even her weird little laugh—but she appreciated the unexpected care her mother was putting into her lessons.

Ridley was also surprised when her mother asked if she could read Ridley some of her writing. Ridley offered thoughtful criticism, and her mother listened and made changes and didn't blow up at her or cause a fuss. (And you know how I feel about *fusses*.) It felt like a miracle.

It felt like magic.

Like Ridley's favorite kind of trick...

Transformation.

One morning, about a month later, it all became clear.

Mrs. Larsen knocked on Ridley's door, opening it just a crack. "Need some help with your stretches?"

"Sure. Thanks, Mom."

Mrs. Larsen pulled a chair to the side of the bed, but instead of sitting and beginning the exercises, she stood there, staring down at her daughter.

"What's wrong?" Ridley asked.

"I have a confession," her mother answered. Her voice sounded oddly thick. "I heard...I mean, I know...that is, I saw everything. In the auditorium. I...was there."

"You...what?"

"I was at the resort, Ridley. When I got home from my appointment, you weren't there...and I was furious because you'd snuck off *again* without telling me... and I came to find you...because I knew you'd be at the resort *again*." Her mother's voice was quivering.

Ridley was shocked. "Are you telling me you were in the auditorium?"

"I saw all these people rushing inside...and I was so scared something was wrong...and I followed...and *there you were*...and I couldn't get to you...and, and, and then I heard you say..."

Her mother's face had gone very red. Ridley was dumbfounded. So many emotions were coursing through her, and she didn't know if she was scared, relieved, or a mix of both. "I...didn't mean..." Ridley started, then drooped in her seat. "I guess I did mean what I said. I'm really sorry, Mom."

"I know," Mrs. Larsen replied, taking a deep breath. "I just...how could you think that?"

Ridley's jaw dropped. She waited for the usual anger to come roaring into her veins, but then she noticed the pain in her mother's eyes. She replayed her mother's question in her mind: *How could you **think** that?*

Did that mean it wasn't true?

"I don't know," Ridley answered, softening. "I just...worry about it sometimes."

"I have a lot on my plate, Ridley...a *lot*. I buy our groceries and make our meals and clean our house and *yes*, I *work*...because someone has to...to keep things afloat. But the one thing I need to make certain

you know is that *you* are not on my plate. You *are* my plate. You are the *reason* I do all these things. I work so hard...because I love you. Right inside here." She pressed her hand against her chest.

"It's hard to see love that's invisible." Ridley's voice was much calmer than she expected. They were finally talking. She didn't want to ruin it.

Mrs. Larsen dabbed at her nose. "You're right... and I'm sorry. I know I often put my writing and my deadlines first....Well, usually the deadlines arrive and *then* the writing follows...at least lately....I'm having a hard time cracking my main character's motivation, you see....Oh my, I'm doing it again, aren't I? The point is...I need to find a better balance."

"Those things are important to you."

"Yes, but so are you. I want you to know that."

Ridley thought of what she'd been through with her friends over the past few months. She thought of the arguments. Of wanting to be right all the time. She had so much more she wished to tell her mother.

That they shared the same kind of anger.

That she'd learned when to fight and when to concede.

What she said was, "You're important to me too, Mom."

Because change can happen when you don't force it.

Because sometimes, love is that simple.

Later, after Ridley's exercises and her bath and her breakfast, she asked her mother if she would join her in the lab.

"What are we doing in here?" asked Mrs. Larsen.

"You're going to help me rebuild the project I took to the inventors' fair," said Ridley. "The one that got smashed."

"I'd like that," her mother answered, wiping her

hands on her freshly ironed pants. "I never got to see the first version." Ridley retrieved the toolbox from the shelf and placed it onto the workbench. "Say," Mrs. Larsen added. "After we're done here, why don't you invite your magical friends over? I feel like we haven't seen them in a while."

Ridley smiled and said, "I'd like that too."

OUR GRAND
— FINALE —

Well, friends, it's just about that time.

What time, you might be asking?

Time for our story to come to an end.

As all stories do.

But first, my final confession.

Have you been wondering exactly who has been sharing these tales of the Magic Misfits with you? Are you willing to guess?

Because I'm willing to bet that your guess is right.

We are all much older now.

What happened to us happened a long time ago.

Like I said, all stories end. We've decided to share our stories with you in the hopes that you will have your own stories to tell. Stories are often just one giant Circle. There are beginnings in endings. And that is what we would like to end this story with. An invitation to begin again.

Mr. Vernon's Magic Circle needs new members to keep it going. We believe that you are worthy. You've got tricks up your sleeve, after all.

I mentioned at the beginning that I'd hoped you've been practicing all the magic I've taught you thus far. (Even if you haven't been, it's never too late to start.)

Join us, won't you? The world will always need a little more magic.

In fact, here's your official invitation (and one final peek into our pasts, before we all move into the future together):

You are cordially invited
to attend the grand opening of
Vernon's Magic Mansion.
Tonight.
Just after sunset.

Take my hand.

We make our way from the Grand Oak Resort, where you've been staying, up the road, away from town and into the woods. Though you're tired from hiking and swimming and horseback riding classes, you still manage to clean up nicely. You're wearing your finest. Maybe it's a tuxedo or maybe a gown. Perhaps it's a glittering green toga. Whatever it is, you've made sure that it sparkles as we pass underneath the streetlights.

The sky is growing dim—that beautiful violet blue that soaks the world in anticipation. The woods are quiet, as if whatever hides in the shadows heard us approaching.

At the end of the driveway, we glance up and see the mansion. Every window glows, beaming amber light across the hilltop. Cars are parked in every available spot. We approach the front door. It's been painted since the last time we were here—bright copper with glossy black trim. The rest of the mansion is an unobtrusive gray, but the door? Someone wanted us to notice this door. It opens as if by itself.

We enter the foyer. The floor shines. A chandelier throws soft glitter across dark wallpaper. Looking closer, you notice the pattern hints subtly at the suits of a deck of cards. From down the hall, we hear murmuring voices. We follow them to a grand room, a place that once might have held spectacular gatherings and that hopes to do so again. It's certainly ready to. These floors have been painted black. The walls and ceiling crimson. Rows of chairs arch around a stage. Red velvet curtains drape across a high proscenium.

A crowd is gathering. You recognize many of their faces, though you've never met any of them officially. You're tempted to say hello. And maybe you will. Later.

The seats are filling up. Take yours near the front. Hurry! The seat is marked RESERVED. Just for you.

As the lights flash, you gaze around in wonder. The murmurs grow as the lights dim, but everyone quiets as they go completely dark. You can feel your heart in your chest, pounding like the engine of a locomotive racing through a tunnel. A spot appears against the curtains—as white and bright as the sun. In the center of the circle stands a man who radiates a familiar warmth. He removes his top hat and flicks aside the front of his cape. Its lining flashes red. The man smiles, his black, pencil-thin mustache stretching across his top lip, just as you've always imagined it would.

"Ladies, gentlemen, everyone," says the man. "Welcome to our new home. And I mean that in the widest sense of the word. *Home.* We've worked hard to create a place where you will feel welcome. Where you will feel wonder. Where you'll find family and friends and conversation. For isn't that what makes a home? You are welcome tonight, of course, but please know, you will always be welcome, as long as these walls stand and probably even if they don't.

"This evening is our grand opening! To help us celebrate, I've gathered six very talented performers for you. They're here to inspire chills, thrills, awe, and wonderment. Though they are young, I see myself in each of them. They've taught me so much over the past few years, I feel like a new man. Tonight, may you feel new as well.

"Without further ado, I give you, my friends, the Magic Misfits!" The man claps and steps aside as the spotlight blinks out and the curtains part.

Six figures stand before you in the new dark, backlit by a cerulean glow. The audience roars as the lights come up. There's Carter, blinking as his blue eyes adjust. His blond hair flops to the side. His dark suit is sharp. His mouth curls as he tries to hold back a grin.

Beside him stands his cousin, Leila, who's dressed in a rainbow sequined skirt and a red jacket with silver cording and sparkling epaulettes. We all hope that her straitjacket will appear shortly. Next are Olly and Izzy holding hands and wearing big, toothy smiles. Their black hair mirrors each other, as do their pink-yellow-and-orange-plaid three-piece suits. Theo rises over them, standing tall and proud. His white tuxedo is a change from what we've usually seen him dressed in, and we like it. At the end is Ridley, her gauzy pink dress ruffled like a flower. It's so unlike her, but we know that's why she's wearing it. She wants to do something unexpected, because that's just her way. Her wild curls and bright eyes tell us that she's still the same girl inside, no matter how she may transform on the outside.

Carter steps forward and raises his hand, thanking the crowd for the applause. "Thank you, Dante," he says loudly into the wings. "We're honored to be here." As he adjusts his jacket, hundreds of playing cards drop to the stage from inside. They keep pouring out, as if there's some sort of card spigot under his arms. "I'll clean those up later," he says with a wink.

Leila twirls and then holds out her hands to the

audience. She claps her palms together, and rainbow streamers shoot from her sleeves and into the first few rows. One of them brushes your cheek.

The twins shout, "*One! Two! Three!*" A moment later, Izzy is perched, standing on Olly's shoulders.

Theo sticks out his tongue and blows a raspberry. From the rear of the theater comes a flapping of wings. Several doves shuttle a violin and a bow over the heads of the audience. We all stare up, nervous and exhilarated, until the birds and the instrument reach Theo safely. He gives a polite bow before glancing to the final Misfit beside him.

Ridley spins her chair in place. When she comes back around, her poufy pink dress has been replaced with a glittering green toga, and the look on her face is filled with secrets. The good kind. The kind that make you wonder, that give you chills, that make you wish to keep turning pages and coming back for more. Ridley calls out, "Have we got a show for you!"

You know she's right. You can't wait to see what they've been practicing, what they've prepared now that they've had time to finally just be themselves. A group of kids who love figuring out how things work, who love sharing what they've learned, who love making people smile.

You realize that you are smiling. Their magic is already here. It's been here all along.

You are ready to join them. To join us.

All you need to do is repeat after me.

SIM SALA BIM!

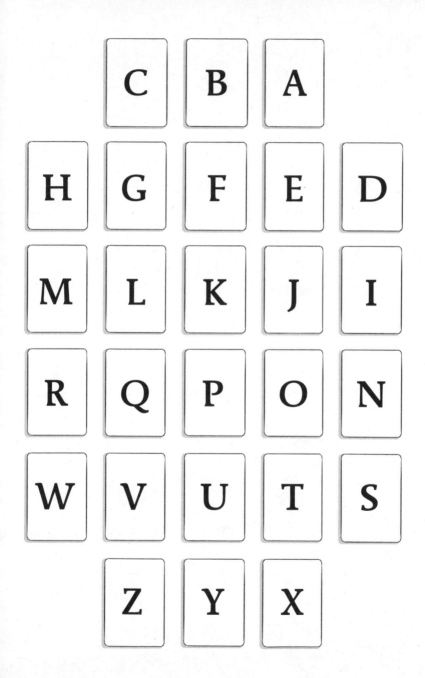

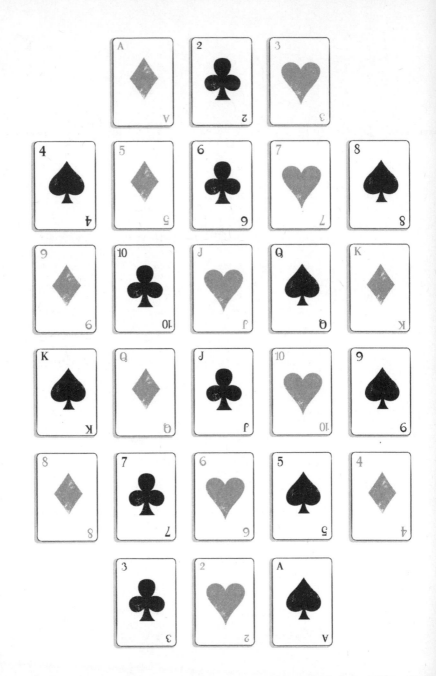

—— ACKNOWLEDGMENTS ——

Sincere thanks to the many people who have helped put *The Fourth Suit* together. As any magician will tell you, a successful illusion show can never happen without a masterful backstage crew. So I offer my heartfelt appreciation to the many, far more talented people than myself who were part of bringing these characters and stories to life, most importantly: Deirdre Jones at Little, Brown Books for Young Readers, for keeping this fast-moving train from careening off its tracks; Dan Poblocki, our unique carnival's ultimate pitchman; Lissy Marlin, whose wonderful images draw crowds in every town; Kyle Hilton, the illustrious Magic Moments illustrator; Laura Nolan, for her elegant whip-cracking skills; Jonathan Bayme, the man behind my magical curtain in books and life; and Timothy Meola, my remarkable assistant and right-hand man—although considering everything he does, he's really also my left-hand man, but since that would leave me handless and unable to type, let's just stick to the right one.

And to all of you who have read this entire series, who have learned the lessons, solved the codes, practiced the tricks, developed a routine...well, that's just, wow, that's fantastic. It's more than I ever imagined a book of my words could accomplish. I'm wholeheartedly humbled and honored that you and magic have become fast friends.